WHERE M'

Strugg

Mark Ingle

Copyright © 2025 Mark Ingle All rights reserved

This novel is considered historical fiction. While some events are based on historical records, other events are fictionalized. Therefore, the characters portrayed in these events are fictitious. Any similarity to real persons, living or dead, is coincidental and not intended by the author.

No part of this book may be reproduced, or stored in a retrieval system, or transmitted in any form or by any means, electronic, mechanical, photocopying, recording, or otherwise, without express written permission of the publisher.

ISBN: 979-8-218-65830-4
ISBN: 979-8-218-65843-4

Cover design by: Mark Ingle
Original Manuscript titled "Where My Heart Leads Me"
Library of Congress Control Number: Txu2468244

INTRODUCTION

"Where My Love Leads Me" explores the turmoil of war and the suffering such conflict can bring to humankind. The reasons for such wars can vary, but the consequences can have lasting effects on human lives. Acts of desperation to win at all costs are often employed to achieve the desired outcome, regardless of the consequences it may bring. Is that not what wars are all about? Winning the desired result. But despite the chaos wars usually bring, love can grow and bloom. Like a flower growing from a crack on a sidewalk. Or creatures living deep on the ocean floor, which scientists seem to think is impossible. Love does find a way in such horrible times, as human emotions play a significant role in love and war. Since both love and war are aspects of human events. And therefore, both human events are put to the test. It tests human nature regarding philosophical, social-political, psychological, and economic endeavors. It provides justification for such human nature.

In war, the fighters will ensure that the bloody conflict is justifiable. Such conflicts are moral in upholding whatever goal suits their endeavors. They will use religion or constitutional authority to support their agenda. Love, on the other hand, is a state of mind where one desires to satisfy their love and emotions without the use of violence. However, this is not always the case. Love and war, which might seem quite different, can sometimes lead to one another. As a result, they are both linked as if they are intertwined like two elements in space. They somehow meet in a dance where one cannot move without the other, as brutal and violent as war can be. One makes the other one possible. Just like a forest fire can cause new trees to sprout. Warfare can bring people together by chance and lead to love.

PROLOGUE

For many years, if not centuries, men have explored and fought for the atomic number 79. Seeking its value and what it could bring to their fortunes. This would be gold. This nuclear element has been widely used for money. Kingdoms and empires have risen and fallen over this precious metal. It draws people together but can also tear them apart. Diamonds can also have the same effect. This solid form of carbon has been traded for value for many years. Both gold and diamonds are high-value items. And when one can find an abundance of either value, it will attract attention. However, gold has a higher liquidity value and is generally easier to buy and sell.

Gold will have many individuals do whatever it takes to obtain it. The excitement and greed for such precious metal will cause people to travel long distances to get it. It's like a wind calling them to it. And when it calls, waves of people follow the wind to mine the gold. This will cause mass migration, like a flock of birds migrating to greener pastures. Some call it a gold rush. First, they hit the stream beds for the gold stuff, and then they prospect to find the veins of lode gold where the source of gold was. And if the gold discovery is vast enough to be considered one of the largest deposits of atomic 79, the effects would cause shock waves. Devastating enough to trigger a war.

And in wars, as in between wars, many people follow a religion based on faith. Faith gives peace and comfort since a spiritual world awaits them when they die. After all, we all will eventually die. If the religion informs its followers to follow a set of rules or lose their chance of receiving divine grace and redemption, they follow what their religion requires. Even if it means denying what the heart seeks, craves, and desires. The followers feel they must act when a religious order directs them to follow a particular course of action.

In a way, the followers fight internal wars in their hearts and minds. They know what their hearts desire but deny it or risk losing their religious sanctity. One person will say that if you have God in your heart, that is all that matters. Others would argue that you can love God in your heart and still have room to love someone you consider your soul mate.

A religious order will say that if you take a solemn vow, your heart can only serve God. If someone practices to honor this vow and still struggles with their human emotions, a battle will develop in their mind and heart. It then becomes a struggle over who controls the heart's destiny. The religion the person practices to serve, or the passion for someone they want to fall in love with. And if the passion for someone exists, can they still love that special someone and serve God with all their heart? If the answer is yes, then are solemn religious vows essential?

CHAPTER 1 – THE BATTLE OF COLENSO

It was December 1899, and the Second Boer War was in its second month. The British fought and lost the First Boer War, in March 1881. In the British defense, they did not put much effort into fighting the Boers the first time in South Africa. Realizing they had lost their battles, the British government gave up two provinces. It was not worth the effort for the mighty British Empire to spend tons of money and send thousands of men to fight in these territories that they considered of low substantial value. So, the Boers won and kept two republics, the Orange Free State and the South African Republic, also known as the Transvaal province. The treaty with the British allowed them to govern the republics as they saw fit. Provided the Boers did not form any partnership with foreign governments, unless first approved by the British government.

Who were the Boers? The word "Boer" means farmer in Dutch. In South Africa, the Boers were predominantly Dutch settlers, sometimes referred to as "Free Burghers," and a minority of settlers from Germany, Scandinavia, and Switzerland.

However, an event happened in 1886 that would change the course of history: "The

Witwatersrand Gold Rush." This gold rush led to the establishment of Johannesburg and paved the way for the mineral revolution in South Africa. However, the vast amount of gold was located in one of the territories that the British government had lost. The British government now realized the territories they lost in the First Boer War were worth something important after all. They also learned that they would have to retake the two republics they had lost in the First Boer War. So, the Boer, along with a small contingency of the Irish Nationalists, joined together to fight the British military one more time.

Two months into the fighting, the battle at Colenso was in full swing, with bloodshed showing no sign of stopping anytime soon.

Colenso is a town on the southern bank of the Tugela River in the KwaZulu-Natal province. The British controlled the province, but Boer commanders managed to infiltrate the area. The town was also strategically located near the central Durban-Johannesburg railway. The British military goal was to provide relief to Ladysmith, which was being besieged by Boer commandos. The Boer commandos' goal was simple enough: keep the British from reaching Ladysmith in the Natal province.

Thousands of various British infantry units marched towards Colenso under heavy artillery fire from the Boers. The British soldiers march quickly and in a close, tight formation.

Several thousand Boer commandos were situated just south of the Thukela River (Tugela), facing the British heading north towards the river. Most Boer men were located on the heights of the Hlongwane Hill and the stone trenches below, armed with their German Mauser Model 1895 rifles. The Mauser was a magazine-fed, bolt-operated rifle that used stripper clips to reload the magazine.

A railway bridge across the Thukela River was the objective of the British to cross the river to capture Colenso. However, the bridge was destroyed a month earlier by the Boer commandoes under the orders of General Joubert.

Near Colenso, British General Sir John Hildyard, in his fifties, sat on his horse and observed his Second Brigade reach Colenso through his field glasses. Next to him were several of his officers, such as Colonel Blagrove and Major Sanders, who were also reviewing the action from their horses. Hildyard's Second Brigade advanced under heavy artillery fire from the General's position.

Several British infantry soldiers were being cut to pieces as a mortar shell exploded near their feet. Several other soldiers were blown away as a cannon shell hit them directly. Yet the men continued their valiant march. From the general's position, another shell made a direct hit on several other British foot soldiers. Cannon smoke was coming from the other side of the Thukela River, where the Boer artillery was positioned. General Hildyard turned to Colonel Blagrove with a grave look as constant artillery continued.

"If those blasted guns keep firing from those heights, our men will never make it out alive."

"Yes, sir. It appears the Boer has ample long-range artillery."

Major Sanders reassured Colonel Blagrove's assessment. "Yes, General. They have about 30 pieces of 1-pounder, 37mm Maxim Vickers, and 75mm Creusots."

General Hildyard replied as he continued to examine the battle through his field glasses. "It appears General Botha came well prepared for Colenso."

Suddenly, a messenger in the name of Lieutenant Smith galloped quickly to the general. They quickly salute each other.

"Yes, what is it, Lieutenant?"

"Pardon, General Hildyard. But I'm here to convey a message from General Hart."

The general was losing his patience. "What?"

"The Irish Fifth Brigade is in the process of retiring, General."

"In what in the devil's name for?"

"The Boers have heavy fortified defenses, General Sir."

"What defenses?"

"They have blocked the ford with barbed wire. And their guns are inflicting heavy losses on the brigade, Sir."

"How many Boers?"

"I least several hundred, Sir."

"Damn! Now, our left flanking position is lost."

Colonel Blagrove added in. "It appears General Hart will need reinforcements, Sir."

Major Sanders, "Should I notify General Buller, Sir?"

General Hildyard took a deep breath and nodded his head in despair. "Yes, Major. You may dispatch the news."

"Very well, Sir."

Major quickly galloped away as General Hildyard turned and looked at the battlefield with his field glasses again.

"Now, Lieutenant. You may go."

Lieutenant Smith began to salute the general as he sat on his horse in a saluting position, awaiting the general's return salute. Colonel Blagrove looked on, wondering if the general would address him. The general addressed the lieutenant while observing the fighting from his field glasses.

"What are you waiting for, Lieutenant?"

Without saying another word, the lieutenant hurriedly galloped away.

A worried look appeared on Colonel Blagrove's face. "Should we lead a second attack when the first one fails?"

Hildyard turned to the colonel with a stern look on his face. "I don't know yet, Colonel! The outcome of the first march has yet to be decided."

"Sorry, Sir. I didn't mean to sound pessimistic."

General Hildyard did not reply as he continued to look at the troops through his field glasses. Down below, towards the Thukela River, another shell sent more bodies flying. Cannon smoke rises from the other side of the Thukela River.

British artillery near General Hildyard's position attempted to fire at the Boer. However, since the Boers occupied the high ground, their artillery fire rained down on the British from the heights above the Thukela River, using 75mm Creusot guns. The Boer sharpshooters also fired down on the British gunners, as several gunners were hit with rifle fire. Bullets tear through the vulnerable British soldiers. One British gunner was shot between the eyes by a Boer bullet. Several gunners abandon their weapons as they run to a nearby dried-up watercourse for cover.

Captain Paff led the Boers from the heights. He observed the British positions from his field glasses. From the captain's position, he saw General Hildyard's Second Brigade being hit with artillery shells as they continued to march forward. Captain Paff went over to a subordinate officer standing nearby.

"I want you to put more fire down on them. I don't want them to cross that river. Do you understand me?"

"Yes, Captain Paff." The officer quickly directed the gunners into action as Paff turned and continued to look at the British positions.

Guns of the Royal Artillery, about 500 meters away from the Boer positions, attempted to fire their 12-pound guns but had difficulty from Boer rifle fire. The Boer sharpshooters have little trouble shooting down the gunners. The rifle fire from Boer commando sharpshooters was in action in an elevated area above the Thukela River.

Smoke rises from the small township in Colenso. Several houses were on fire. Various people try in vain to put out the fire. However, their cause appears hopeless as the fire quickly spreads.

A young mother ran with her ten-year-old son hand in hand as they tried to avoid incoming shelling from a Boer position. Suddenly, a shell explodes nearby as they run to a nearby chapel. Luckily, both escaped injury as they ran into the chapel.

A small group of Boer officers looked down on the British positions from a high ground. A few use their field glasses. One of them is General Louis Botha, and the other is Major De Jager. General Botha turned to De Jager.

"Major De Jager. Go inform the batteries to be careful not to fire down on the town. Our objective is the British infantry, not innocent women and children. Do I make myself clear, Major?"

"Yes, General Botha. I will see to it."

Without another word, the major quickly left as he went to his horse nearby. An aide was holding the horse's rein. De Jager promptly

CHAPTER 1 – THE BATTLE OF COLEN...

climbed into his saddle and galloped away. Meanwhile, the rest of the officers, including General Botha, continued to survey the British positions.

Several wounded Boer soldiers were being carried off on stretchers as an artillery shell exploded near them, some distance away. One of the Boer soldiers cried in pain from his severe wounds.

A Boer commando shouts, "Get them to the medics!"

A wagon cart arrived to carry the wounded. The wounded soldiers were placed in an open wagon nearby, which was being used as an ambulance. The wagon quickly left. However, no more than several minutes later. Another shell went off from the British artillery. The blast destroyed the wagon, killing every soldier on the wagon but one who managed to crawl.

The Boer commando cries, "We need a medic! Now!"

Another Boer commando replied, "The medic is dead."

Fear and horror were painted on the Boer faces. More shells whistle through the air.

On the heights above the Thukela River, another group of Boer sharpshooters fired their rifles down on the marching British. A field cornet named Fourie then suddenly walked hurriedly behind the Boer sharpshooters.

"How are you boys holding up?"

A Boer soldier turned and addressed the field cornet. "Fine, Sir."

"How is your ammo?"

Another Boer soldier addressed the field cornet from his firing position. "Ammunition is holding up, Sir."

"Good." Field Cornet smiled at the sharpshooters as they continued the firing. He barks at the shooters.

"Continue, boys. Continue your fire!"

A group of Boer sharpshooters in another area nearby fired from their positions. From their advantageous point, British troops continue the march despite enduring heavy losses. Various British infantry units fell apart as they were cut down by rifle fire.

From a panoramic view of the battlefield, a bright, intense sun bears down on it. Artillery shells exploded everywhere, causing fire and smoke to rise and swell.

CHAPTER 2 – DIANA

The nuns of the Sisters of Hope convent were nestled in the Connacht province in Ireland. The convent has been around for years. During such times, the convent had experienced wars, famine, and national conflicts. The convent housed around a hundred nuns and novitiates. The Sisters of Hope focus on a life of prayer, contemplation, and Christian religious service to God by taking vows of chastity and obedience to the church's guidelines. Within the walls, the nuns live and practice their religious faith. And those in training, called novitiates, also live in the convent. They prepare to become a nun by studying and learning the role before taking their official vows to become one.

In her sixties, Mother Theresa was the Superior Mother of the convent. It was the middle of January 1900, and she sat behind her oak-finished desk, writing a letter. She wore the traditional robe, headdress (veil), and a silver crucifix around her neck. Her office was immaculate, with pictures of the Virgin Mary and Jesus Christ hanging on the wall. Mother Theresa ran the convent of the Sisters of Hope with the zeal of a military officer. The letter was to her immediate superior, the Catholic Bishop of Ireland, Bishop Michaels. Her letter concerned the conduct of Diana Ryan, who was still a novitiate at the convent. The letter was as follows:

"To my most reverend Bishop Michaels, of this Blessed day, January Fifteen of the first year of our new century. As you know, I have worked diligently as a sister of faith for many years, as a dedicated servant for the causes our order holds so dear. As I begin a new year as Mother Superior, I will continue to dedicate my life to ensure my Sisters are well acquainted with the obligations of religious life as a Sister of Hope. Every novitiate represents a clear case of judgment concerning acceptance into the Sisterhood. However, I have a novitiate named Diana Ryan, whom you met at our charitable event concerning the orphans last spring. Although young, she shows remarkable maturity in dealing with the unfortunate. Her presence seems to light up the faces of those seeking spiritual guidance, our holy order can bestow."

Theresa momentarily stops writing as she is lost in thought. She continued.

"However, Sister Diana at times displays a lack of order in her affairs with those outside the convent. Her zeal for life bubbles over with high bursts of energy, which sometimes cannot be contained. She does not adhere ----."

Suddenly, she heard a knock at the door. Mother Theresa continued her writing. "Yes?"

Sister Francis, who just turned thirty, opened

the door. Excitement painted her face. She cautiously moved a few steps into the office. Mother Theresa looked up.

"What seems to be the trouble, Sister?"

"It's Sister Diana, Mother Superior!"

"What has our beloved child done now?"

"She is fraternizing and dancing with the beggars in front of the convent."

Without saying a word, Theresa immediately stood and quickly walked to the doorway. A look of dread came across her face. She left her office, following Francis.

From the convent's second-floor balcony, Theresa and Francis looked down toward the street in front of the convent. To their amazement, they saw Sister Diana dancing in front of several homeless men, one of whom was playing the bagpipes.

Sister Diana, at twenty-three, was dressed in her white novitiate habit and dancing in front of several homeless men. One sat on the curb by the side of the street. Diana was a beauty with slender hips. Her hair was hardly visible under the habit she must wear. The men clapped along to a bagpiper standing near them as Diana danced a jovial Irish jig. She picked up her robe with one hand, revealing her ankles, while her other hand was raised over her head, twisting about. Her feet and hips sway in perfect rhythm to the bagpipe music. A small group of pedestrians stopped to enjoy the scene. They joined the homeless men clapping and tapping their feet as Diana continued dancing away.

Theresa and Francis stared at the spectacle in shock.

A discordant look ran over Theresa's face, "This is truly unbecoming of Sister Diana!"

Francis echoed her sentiment. "She will surely enter the lake of fire."

"So, it's exercise she seeks. I shall give her exercise. Have Sister Diana report to the kitchen immediately."

"Yes, Mother Theresa."

Theresa left. Francis stayed longer on the balcony, somewhat taken by Diana's dancing.

Theresa called to her. "Are you coming, Sister Francis?"

"Yes, Mother Theresa." Francis quickly left.

It was nightfall, and Diana, the sole occupant of the kitchen, was on her hands and knees, wearing an apron over her habit. She vigorously rubbed the floor with a rag. Beside her was a bucket of soapy water. She stopped and ran a hand over her forehead, wiping the perspiration. Sister Catherine, a spiritual trainee in her early twenties, entered and stopped before Diana.

"I see you are hard at work. And at this wee hour, too. Should you not be preparing for prayer and then bed?"

Diana continued her scrubbing without looking up. "If the hour is so late, why are you here?"

"I came for Sister Agatha's rosary. You know how forgetful she can be. Besides, it serves you right. All that dancing and making a nuisance of yourself..."

Diana interrupted, "Thank you for your wisdom, Sister Catherine."

Catherine then began to sing.
> "You cannot fool Mother Theresa
> She knows everything that we do
> If you think that you can fool her
> You will just get yourself in trouble
>
> So, give up, Miss Gypsy Dancing Queen
> It is not welcome at the Sisters of Hope
> Instead, focus on your devotion and duties
> Because you can never fool Mother Theresa."

While on the floor scrubbing, Diana answered back as she sang.
> "I understand what you say
> Duties and devotion to our Lord
> But when the spirit moves, I shall be
> Like a bird spreading its wings."

Diana stopped scrubbing the floor as she stood. She threw her rag in the bucket. She continued her singing.
> "I dance for the Lord on high
> Move as if dancing with wings
> To the beat of the music in me

For my soul takes me where I want to be."

She began to dance, moving around on the floor. Her dancing was graceful and energetic, mixing her steps like a dancing queen. She then mocked Catherine with a playful laugh as she continued her dancing. She then stopped. She smiled and winked at her.

Catherine, in turn, shook her head disapprovingly. "Mother Theresa is counting the days before she's through with you." Catherine sang.

> "You cannot fool Mother Theresa
> She knows everything that we do
> If you think that you can fool her
> You will just get yourself in trouble
> Miss Dancing Gypsy Queen."

Catherine glanced around. She moved over and retrieved the rosary at the counter. She walked over to Diana. "Do not work too long, Sister Diana. You are going to need your knees for fasting and prayer tomorrow." Catherine left the kitchen.

Diana waved off Catherine as she smirked. "What does she know?" Diana then went back on her hands and knees and continued scrubbing away. Suddenly, Diana recalled one of her past unrestrained lives before she entered the sisterhood.

It was nightfall, and Diana's adoptive parents were fast asleep in their modest home. They lived in a small town in Ireland, not far from Limerick. She was nineteen at the time. With her lengthy hair, she wore a low-cut black saloon-style dress that was very flattering on her. She slipped out of her bedroom window and hurried away from her parents' house, cutting down a dark road.

Diana's recollection then led her to a saloon. It was a local Irish pub. Diana danced on the top of the bar while the bartender and his male customers stared at her in delight. She kicked up her heels, and pulled up her skirt, exposing her legs, knee-high. The men clapped as she carried on. She moved with grace and form, a true natural. Her long hair flew in the air as she twirled and stomped her feet to the Irish music played by a show-stopping fiddle player.

The vivacious Diana now sat at a table with a group of men around her in the saloon. She attempted to drink a pint of Irish beer in one swallow. But she could not. She ended up spewing the beer to the laughter of the men.

Later in the saloon, Diana played cards with some of the men at a table. Several of them became a little too friendly with her. They pinch her and place their hands on her thighs. Diana brushed them away with a smile that did not offend. She continued having fun without being overly friendly.

It was quite late, and a buggy driven by the Irish saloon Owner, O'Malley, with Diana next to him in her black saloon-style dress, approached her family's house. O'Malley was in his fifties, heavy-set, and had several days of hair on his face. He turned to her, grinning.

"Well. Here we are, Diana."

"You won't tell my parents, Mr. O'Malley."

"Of course not." He placed a hand on one of her thighs. "Your father and I go back many years. But this secret I will keep."

Diana politely removed his hand from her thigh.

"If only you did not remind me of my daughter Sara. The things I could do with you."

Diana smiled as she exited the buggy and turned to him. "Thank you for the ride, Mr. O'Malley." She began to walk but stopped and turned to him. "And to let you know. I would not partake in your delusional fantasy if you were the last man on this here island. Goodnight, Sir." She turned and continued to walk to her adoptive parents' house.

A look of displeasure registered on his face. He grabbed the reins. "Get up." His carriage pulled away. Diana made her way back to her bedroom window, and her reminiscence ended.

She looked up with her hands and knees. "Maybe I am a dancing gypsy queen." A sensual smile came over her. "Oh well." She continued to scrub the floor.

The following day was a clear but somewhat cold afternoon with several sisters in the cultivated area at the convent. The area was home to a diverse range of vegetation. The sisters wore their usual work clothes with their coats because of the cool weather, retrieving beets from the ground as they grasped the beet plants at the base of the leaves. Because the ground was somewhat hardened, they used a garden fork to loosen the soil around the beet's root. They also sported gloves and placed the beets in wooden baskets. Besides Diana, there were Catherine, Agatha, Dorothy, and Adeline. Agatha and Dorothy, in their gold-rimmed glasses, were in their 50s, while Adeline appeared to be in her early 30s. Each sister was hard at work, with Diana, Dorothy, and Adeline doing the picking. Meanwhile, Catherine and Agatha loaded the beets into the baskets. They engaged in their daily conversation.

Agatha spoke, "I don't believe our Holiness..." Suddenly, she stopped speaking as they all performed the sign of the cross in respect of the pope. She continued. "...Has any indication of changing his position on this Americanism movement sweeping our continent like a bitter cold wind. It brings chills to our spiritual prosperity."

Dorothy interjected, "The movement is gaining popularity in France. And my I dear say, even Italy."

The news took Adeline. "At the Vatican City steps?"

"Yes. But our Holiness..." Again, like clockwork, Agatha stopped speaking, as they all performed a quick sign of the cross. She continued. "...Will stand firm. You wait and see. Our Holiness..." She momentarily paused as they all performed a quick sign of the cross. "...Will fight the evil which has taken hold."

"However, Sister Agatha. This movement is simply a form of democracy. And I do not see democracy as such a bad thing."

"My dear Sister Adeline. You do not see the danger of separating governmental affairs from religious duties?"

Catherine nodded in disapproval. "It appears Sister Adeline needs prayer for spiritual guidance."

Dorothy smiled, "I will pray for our Sister tonight."

Agatha continued with her religious point of view. "For centuries, our history was shaped by religious teachings brought by our church. And to see our teachings is now controlled by these so-called modern ideas. It is an abomination!"

Dorothy raised her hands, "Yes, Sister Agatha!"

Agatha paused and took several breaths. "The work can be somewhat taxing."

Dorothy smiles, "God's work is not meant to be easy, Sister."

"I am not complaining. I am simply stating a fact."

"It sounds like a complaint to me."

Catherine appeared agitated. "Stop it at once, all of you. There is no room for complaining as we complete the work of our Holiness." The nuns all stopped and performed the sign of the cross. "...We should be thankful for this day."

Dorothy smiled reassuringly, "And we are, Sister Catherine."

Agatha turned to Diana. "Sister Diana, you have been unusually quiet today. Is something concerning you, my child?"

Catherine replied, "Her mind wanders to her dancing from the other evening. Does it not, Sister Diana?"

Catherine and Adeline let out a giggle.

Agatha was surprised by the news. "Oh, my child! Were you dancing again?"

Diana smiled and continued to pull the beets.

"I say. She made Mother Superior blooming mad."

"Now, Sister Adeline, mind your business."

Catherine injects, "Had her washing floors all night long."

Sister Agatha shook her head in disgust. "When are you going to learn, Sister Diana? You cannot fool with Mother Nature, and you cannot fool Mother Theresa."

Adeline nodded in agreement. "That's the truth."

"I only did it to cheer up the homeless lads. Are not the Sisters of Hope to give comfort to the less fortunate?"

Agatha gives Diana a smile. " So, it was comfort, my child. Yes, we must reach out to those less fortunate."

Catherine raised her eyebrows, "But for

heaven's sake, not dancing! Especially not in a public street wearing the habit. If it's dancing you want, visit the saloons."

"Now, Sister Catherine, ease your anger. Our Sister's heart was in the right place."

"Her heart, perhaps, but not her head."

"I have been meaning to ask you, Sister Diana. How did you learn how to dance?"

Diana replied to Agatha with a childlike smile, "I suppose you could say it came to me naturally."

Suddenly, Sister Adeline looks the other way. "Sister Francis is waving for us to come in."

Dorothy looked at her watch. "It's time for our rosary."

Agatha reached over and touched Diana's arm. "Just remember, Sister Diana, to seek the Lord before all your doings."

"Yes, Sister Agatha."

Diana, Dorothy, and Adeline helped Catherine and Agatha with the baskets full of beets.

CHAPTER 3 – THE LETTER

Near Ladysmith, South Africa, Major John MacBride, in his 40s, dressed in his military gear, sat on a makeshift desk. He commanded about 500 Irish and Irish-American commandos fighting against the British, called the Irish Transvaal Brigade. They were miners who were living in Transvaal and were willing to fight the British. A kerosene lamp provided the only light. A western-style brim cowboy hat with an attached feature pin lay beside him. He was writing a letter. Artillery can be heard firing off in the distance as he continued.

"As you read in the papers, war has begun in South Africa. My men are with other Boer commandos laying siege to Ladysmith against the British forces. This war will surely take its toll on the men, women, and children in the Orange State Free and Transvaal Republics. The British are determined to take their liberties away and give them back to the Uitlanders…."

Two weeks later, Mother Theresa received the MacBride letter and continued reading it in her office with great interest.

"…I know your order does not promote war, and I do not wish to impose such issues on the Sisters of Hope.

However, the Sisters of Hope actively provide medical aid for the Red Cross. Some of my men from the Irish Transvaal Brigade are from your parish. And I know a comforting face from your Sisters will bring up their Irish spirits. Therefore, your utmost assistance is sorely needed. I will provide arrangements upon your Sister's arrival in Pretoria. A base hospital is there, and your Sisters will be aiding the Dutch Red Cross. Although, as you well know, I cannot predict how long this war will last. May God bless you. Yours truly, Major McBride."

Theresa raised her head, lost in thought. She stared at the letter still in her hand. Then, suddenly, she looked up with a smile on her face.

Later that night, several modest single beds lined up against a wall in the convent's sleeping quarters. They were the sleeping quarters for Diana and two other sisters, Alice and Barbara. A kerosene lamp on the wall and a single candle on a dresser provided the only light. Like Diana, Alice, and Barbara were young and still in their novitiate stage. Alice and Barbara, wearing their gowns, were in bed. Alice appeared already asleep while Barbara was still awake. Diana stood before a dresser mirror in her full-length gown as she brushed her hair.

"Sister Diana. When are you going to stop brushing your blooming hair? You know we have to wake early."

"Oh, hush, Sister Barbara. You know I like

brushing a hundred strokes before bed."

Suddenly, with her eyes closed, Alice answered." You both hush. I'm trying to get some sleep."

Barbara turned to Alice. "I thought you were asleep?"

"I would be if both of you commence on sleeping."

Diana stopped brushing. "Well. I'm finished." Diana laid the brush on the dresser counter. She walked over and reached for a metal plate on a small table below the kerosene lamp on the wall. With the plate in hand, she reached for the glass lamp and put out the light. She laid the plate on the table and walked over to her bed.

"Don't forget your prayers, Sister Diana."

"I ready perform my prayers, Sister Barbara."

"And where was I, may I ask?"

Diana reached the bed as she pulled the bed sheets over.

"Indulging in the shower with your whimsical singing."

Barbara sounded a little disappointed. "I see."

"Good night, Sister Barbara."

"You too, Sister Diana."

All three sisters fell fast asleep. Diana's face revealed that she was quite tranquil in her sleep.

Diana then had a dream. She recalled an argument she had while she was living with her adoptive parents. Diana had just turned twenty and was studying for a nursing exam behind her desk in a bedroom. Suddenly, her adoptive mother, Anna, came marching in. She was in her forties and was Diana's mother's sister. She and her husband took custody of Diana after her parents died in a tragic accident.

"I told you to stop your dancing foolery and flirting with the older men. Especially the married ones."

Diana looked up from her textbooks. "What are you talking about?"

"O'Malley. That's who."

Diana did not say a word. Her silence said it all.

"He told your father about your shenanigans at his saloon. How many times have I told you to stop? One of these days, you are going to get yourself in trouble. And neither your father nor I will be there to save your ass."

"You mean my adopted dad."

Anna then slammed the door and approached Diana. "We support you and pay for your nursing education, which ain't cheap."

Diana just sat and listened.

"The agreement was for you to finish your schooling and spend some time at the nunnery."

"I don't want to go to the nunnery."

"Mother Theresa at the sisterhood agreed to take you in. You will just have to be there for a while."

"And how long is that?"

"When your father and I are convinced, you are a changed person. That you'll flirtatious and wild-spirited dancing ways at the local saloons are

CHAPTER 3 – THE LETTER

finished. That some moral fiber has been instilled in you."

"And suppose I don't change?"

"Then I guess you will always stay a nun."

Anna then proceeded to exit as she opened the door. But she stared back at Diana. "And one more thing. If you dance one more time at one of the salons. We are cutting you off. "

She then slammed the door behind her as she left. Diana just sat there and moaned.

Her dream ended as she moved her head back and forth in her sleep.

The following morning, Diana knelt and was about to begin her morning prayers with the other nuns in her sleeping quarters when Catherine hurried over to her.

"Sister Diana. Mother Theresa wishes to see you immediately."

Diana looked up, nervously. The others stared at her. "Do you know why?"

"No."

Without saying another word, Diana followed Catherine, and they left together.

In the Superior's Mother's Office, Theresa was at her desk going through some paperwork as she was writing. She heard a knock on the door.

"Yes."

Diana opened the door.

"Yes, come in, Sister Diana."

Diana closed the door behind her. She walked

over and sat on a chair about across from Theresa. With Diana looking on, Theresa continued to write and shuttled some paperwork as if Diana were not present. A few moments later, she decided to stop what she was doing and laid the work down on her desk.

Theresa began her conversation with a polite smile.

"You are wondering why I have called to see you, Sister Diana?"

"Yes, Mother Superior."

"I call you in because of some urgent matter that has developed in the Orange Free State and the Transvaal Boer republics. As you probably know, another war has broken out between the British and the Boers. Needless to say, events there are in a terrible state. The Boers are in dire need of medical help. They are fighting against huge odds." Theresa paused as she took on a more serious look. "Not to say, this convent is taking sides on this matter. But some of our Irish lads are fighting for the Boers. And as Sisters of Hope, we always extend a hand to our parishioners no matter where they may be. We also actively aid the International Red Cross in providing medical aid to those less fortunate."

Diana stared at Theresa with confusion on her face. Theresa returned her daunting stare with a smile. "The fact of the matter is. I'm sending you and several other sisters to the Boer Republic a week from today. Pretoria, to be exact."

"The South African Republic?"

"If you want to call it that."

"For how long?"

"I suppose for the duration of the war. Or until your services are no longer required."

"But Mother Superior, my vows are in six months."

"Is your life not set aside to honor the obedience in becoming a nun for God's work?"

"Why yes, Mother Theresa."

"Don't you want to become a nun?"

"With all my heart, Mother Theresa. But I'll be the only novitiate on this missionary trip."

"That is true. But you have a formal education as a nurse."

"Yes."

"Then you shall go. You are the only one here with formal nursing training. The Boers are in urgent need of your talents."

"But Mother Superior..."

"I have seen you helping those with therapeutic needs. And I must say, you are quite good." Theresa looked down on her paper and continued to write again. "A Red Cross ship will be docking in Southampton this time next week." She looked up at Diana. "There is no need to argue, Sister Diana. The decision has been made."

Diana sat, stunned in silence.

"Sisters Dorothy, Adeline, Helen, Elizabeth, and Gertrude will accompany you on the trip. When you come back, you will be permitted to take your vows. I am also assigning you the black tunic for this trip. You only wear it when you are with the other sisters. When you return, you will receive a permanent one after taking your vows. Understood?"

"Yes, Mother Theresa. But how about my novitiate tunic?"

"Just take it with you." She grinned," Who knows, it might come in handy."

Diana was puzzled by her last words. Mother Theresa then waved Diana to the door. Diana stood and went to the door. But Mother Theresa gave her one more piece of information before she left.

"Sister Francis will prepare you and the others for this missionary extremity." Theresa smiled, "That is all."

Diana stepped outside as she closed the door behind her.

Theresa smiled. "There goes the dancing, gypsy."

CHAPTER 4 – SAIL AWAY

It was a clear and beautiful day in early February in Southampton, England's harbor. The International Red Cross hospital ship Princess of Wales was docked there. The propeller ship was a one-funnel steam engine, approximately 500 feet long. It was white with a Red Cross painted over its side. It is the only worthy ship the Red Cross had available to send several hundred medical volunteers from Europe to the Second Anglo-Boer War conflict in South Africa.

A crowd of passengers walked up the dock to the ship, carrying their small luggage. A ship crane loaded the heavier items. Diana and the other Irish nuns entered the ship wearing their black habits at its main entrance. Accompanying Diana were Dorothy, Adeline, and Helen, who was in her 40s and overweight; Elizabeth, in her mid-30s, a large-framed woman; and Gertrude, in her early 60s, with a medium-framed build wearing spectacles. Although Gertrude was the oldest hand-picked nun to venture to South Africa, Dorothy was regarded as the leader.

Entering the ship deck, the Irish nuns, led by Dorothy, greeted various passengers as they headed for their quarters. They said their good mornings with smiles on their faces. The ship appeared to be filled, with everyone moving about. Walking behind Dorothy, Helen appeared agitated by what she saw around her.

Dorothy says hello to a ship hand. "Hello---."

Helen interrupted her. "This ship seems a wee bit too crowded, don't you think?"

Dorothy continued to greet those passing with a pleasant smile. "We are here to do God's will, Sister Helen. There is room for all."

Helen did not reply as they continued walking to their quarters.

The nuns entered their quarters, which were nothing more than a ward. Since there were no patients abroad, the ward served as their sleeping quarters for the medical passengers. The long, narrow bunk beds were separated by wooden partitions that offered no privacy. The nuns selected the area where they were to sleep and placed their belongings on wooden shelves in front of the beds.

Helen, who constantly complains, voiced her concerns: "I thought we would have private sleeping quarters."

Dorothy addressed her. "Not on a hospital ship. We are on a mission of mercy. Not a travel excursion."

"I will sleep on the top bed."

I'm afraid that will be for Sisters Diana and Adeline. They're more limber, Sister Gertrude."

In her usual festive mood, Elizabeth said, "This is going to be an exciting trip!"

"Pipe down, will you! This suits you perfectly if you enjoy traveling like animals on a circus ship."

"I hope your bickering will not be part of our everyday routine on this voyage, Sister Helen."

Adeline added her sentiment. "She's always that way, Sister Dorothy."

"I am not."

Dorothy laid a small bag on the bed. "Remember Sisters. We came here to do the Lord's will. Now, I will sleep on this portion. Sister Helen, you will sleep before me, while Sister Elizabeth sleeps behind me. And Sister Gertrude will sleep behind Sister Elizabeth."

"And Sister Diana and me will sleep on top."

Helen found an opportunity to correct Adeline's grammar. "It's Sister Diana, and I who will sleep on the top."

"Sister Diana. You have anything to add?"

"Not me, Sister Dorothy."

"Good."

"I would like to go on deck later and catch up on some reading."

"I thought you would be working on your crocheting, Sister Gertrude?"

"Will that too. But first, I must finish the last chapter on the skill of growing orchids."

"Orchids?"

"Yes, Sister Dorothy. When we finish our duties in South Africa, I will petition Mother Theresa to grow orchids in the garden."

Helen laughs sarcastically. "Mother Theresa will never allow such a thing."

Adeline challenging Helen. "And why not?"

"There is simply no room for such specimens."

Dorothy continued to assert herself as the leader. "We will discuss such topics later. I suggest we unpack and make our way around the ship."

Elizabeth is all smiles. "That sounds like a good idea."

Diana observed several other nuns unpacking a short distance away. "I wonder what sisterhood they represent?"

The other nuns turn in the direction of Diana's stare.

Dorothy provided the answer. "I believe they are from the Francisca Order. But I'm not quite sure."

"Well, that is one topic we can discuss at the dinner." Helen then looked around, as if searching for something. "When is dinner?"

"Like I said. We shall unpack first. Remember, we are on this ship to render our services to the British, for this is a British-run vessel. We make no mention of the Boers. Do you all understand?"

The nuns agreed with Dorothy as they nodded.

Later in the day, everyone sat for dinner in the ship's wardroom mess section. There were long tables nicely lined side by side. Various passengers (medical volunteers) and British military officers sat and enjoyed their meal, as the kitchen helped serve the food. The Irish nuns sat together on one of the tables. Besides the nuns, were two other people. Dorothy sat next to a gentleman named Pierre in his late 50s. Pierre was a doctor by trade in France. He was wearing a suit and sported a mustache. A British nurse named Martha, also in her 50s, sat alongside Diana. Adeline sat on Diana's other side. Martha, sporting a shawl and wearing spectacles, was a retired nurse from England. Dorothy and Pierre were conversing, as the other tables were engaged in their own personal talk.

"I assure you, madam. I mean... Sister Dorothy. The people of France no more care for heresy than the sisters in your convent."

"How is your chicken soup, Doctor Pierre?"

"Needs a little seasoning. But quite fine otherwise."

"Yes, I know, our Excellency, can at times move in slow ways. But our convent do not doubt his true sincerity and selflessness."

"I didn't realize the Sisters of Hope took an active role in helping the Red Cross in times of war."

"Oh! Our sisterhood has a long and distinguished history in helping the Red Cross with assistance when asked." Dorothy tasted her soup. "How long have you practiced medicine in Paris?"

"Thirty years, to be exact." Pierre tasted his

soup. "Tell me, Sister Dorothy, which are you for? The English or the Boers?

"The Sisters of Hope do not take political sides, Doctor Pierre. Our calling is for humanity."

Pierre looks at her dubiously. "But surely. You have an opinion on this issue. Almost everyone on this ship has a point of view on this delicate matter."

Elizabeth sat next to Dorothy, interrupted. "Excuse me, Sister Dorothy. But can you pass me the salt?"

Without saying a word, Dorothy handed the salt container to Elizabeth. Elizabeth frantically sprinkled the salt into her bowl of soup, as if her life depended on it.

Dorothy continued. "I know the English and the Boers have been having problems for a long time now. No doubt, the Uitlanders have been complaining about their treatment ever since the Boers won their freedom to set up their independence from Great Britain."

"In the Uitlanders. You mean the English settlers? No."

"Yes."

"So, is the British government's presence to aid the Uitlanders?"

"And to colonize the Boer republics again. Of course, the Uitlanders want their share of wealth and political influence just like the Boers."

"But South Africa belongs to everyone."

"Yes. But as far as I'm concerned, whoever controls the diamonds and gold should throw it all in the ocean and end this blooming war!"

Pierre laughed at Dorothy's remarks. "It's been said that money is the root of all evil."

"Indeed."

Diana, Adeline, and Martha conversed at the other end of the table. Helen sat nearby. But she was too busy reading a book and eating her food to engage in idle conversation, as she made annoying faces hearing them talk.

"Well. Sister Adeline has been a nun for three years now. Isn't that right, Sister Adeline?"

"Yes, that is right, Sister Diana. "

"And how about you, my dear?"

"Well. I'm not a nun yet."

"What do you mean?"

"Sister Diana is implying that she has not received her vows yet."

"Oh, I see."

"But Mother Theresa said I will receive my vows when we return from the war."

"This Mother Theresa. Is she a kind lady?"

"Oh, why yes. She's very fair."

Adeline reaffirmed. "Very fair indeedy."

"I didn't mean to sound as if I was addressing her so unkindly. But I was raised as a Protestant. The Church of England. So, I haven't had the pleasure to become acquainted with the sisterhood."

"No offense taken, ma'am. My parents were both Protestants, too?"

"And which faith were they in?"

"I rightly don't know, ma'am. They never told me."

"But you went to church with your parents?"

Adeline nods, "Hmm. Hmm." Adeline continued to bite into her meatloaf.

A puzzling look came over Martha's face at Adeline's response. She turned to Diana. "Diana. Why send you away if you were so close to becoming a nun?"

"Diana is a trained nurse."

"Oh! I just retired from nursing. I was a charge nurse at a London hospital."

Diana remarked, "Do you miss being a nurse? Being retired and all."

"Heavens no. Being a nurse in London was a complete zoo. I mean, don't misunderstand. I enjoyed my profession. But after a while, it becomes too laborious. If you know what I mean. Oh, I'm sorry. You were never a nurse. Correct?"

"I studied and did my training at the University College Dublin before I joined the sisterhood."

"Why did you choose it? If you don't mind me asking."

"Well. Nursing, as you know, is a time-honored

profession. Giving aid to the sick...."

Martha interrupted, "I meant the sisterhood?"

"It pleases me to help those in need. Which keeps me limber on my feet."

"Speaking of limber... You should see her dance."

"Oh? You dance, do you?"

"And not ballroom dancing. I mean real Irish dancing. Wild and spirited. I tell you; it's like some gypsy spirit. I have never seen anything like it. It's like something is possessing her."

Diana tried to conceal the sheepish grin on her face." Sister Adeline!"

Helen decided to interject. "The devil possessed her."

Adeline took offense, "How dare you, Sister Helen!"

Helen responded with a smirk as she continued reading.

"Never mind her, Sister Adeline."

Martha touched her hand. "You're a born dancer, I take it?"

Diana smiled beautifully but provided no other response.

A young waiter interrupted their conversation. "More tea?"

Martha nodded, "Yes."

The waiter began refilling the tea glasses, starting with Martha. He worked his way around the table as they continued their conversation.

"I would like to have the pleasure of seeing you dance one day, my dear."

"The sisterhood does not take too kindly to that, ma'am."

"Oh. And why not?"

"We're Sisters of Hope. Dedicated to serving the Lord."

Helen added, "She is not a nun. She wouldn't understand."

"There is nothing wrong with dancing. Why King David praised and danced for our Lord."

"Well, we're not Kings' ma'am. Just nuns. And Irish nuns at that."

Diana and Martha responded with laughter at Adeline's remark. Helen ignored them as she remained glued to her book.

Diana could not sleep the following night as she sat on a recliner on the ship's deck. Hardly anyone else was there. Bright moonlight shone down on her. The moonlight proved sufficient light as she wrote a letter to the nuns in the convent. *"A week has gone by, and we miss you, Sisters, one and all. But we have managed to have a wonderful time onboard the ship..."*

As she wrote, she remembered Adeline, Elizabeth, and her in the ship's lounge area during the day, playing shuffleboard on deck. And then, Helen on a recliner, reading a book. And another with Helen vigorously arguing with two other persons on the deck as Gertrude looked on in amusement. There was Dorothy playing the piano in the ship's lounge area as Diana, Elizabeth, and Adeline sang for a small group of passengers standing around them. They ended their singing to the appreciation of the festive group. Another time, there was Gertrude again sitting in her chair on deck, knitting as she performed crochet-knitting work.

She continued to write:

"...One cannot imagine the magnificent beauty of the sea until one has been out on an extended voyage. The touch of fresh sea wind blowing in your face is divine."

In this passage, Diana reflected on Adeline, Elizabeth, and herself, looking out from the deck during the day toward the beautiful sea, conversing and laughing. The sea breeze tickled their faces. Those happy moments lingered in her mind as she continued to write.

"...I am beginning to realize how small we are when compared to this mighty ocean."

Diana then recalled being on the ship's bow, cutting through the sea like a knife.

The memory of the seagulls caused her to write the following:

"...There is plenty to do onboard. Not one day goes by without a new and wonderful experience."

Diana then pictured Adeline, Elizabeth, and herself on deck, feeding seagulls with pieces of bread. Diana, Adeline, and Elizabeth placed the bread on their hands and laid their arms over the deck railing as the birds came in and picked on the bread. One of the birds landed on the railing and stood before Diana. The bird just sat and waited patiently for Diana to offer him some bread. She does this by pulling her hand in front of the bird. To her amazement, the bird gently picks up the bread from Diana's hand.

"...*Oh, it is so beautiful it simply takes your breath away. Of course, we cannot jump and swim with the habitats.*"

The habitats Diana was writing about were a school of dolphins skipping across the sea's surface at nightfall, being observed by the nuns on deck.

Diana then recalled her dancing, as she wrote, "*And the sea has a way of letting me release energy to lighten the spirits of others. To cheer them up.*" She chuckled. "*But in a positive way, of course.*"

And there was Diana in the lounge area of the ship during the day. Many people, including Pierre and Martha, stood and clapped their hands as she danced to their delight. With her black habit, she danced around. Her dancing covered almost the entire area as she moved gracefully and effortlessly. It was a kind of Irish folk-like dancing, as a passenger played the bagpipes in the background. But Helen and Dorothy were not sociable with Diana's performance, especially

CHAPTER 4 – SAIL AWAY

Helen, who covered her eyes in humiliation.

Diana finished her letter and decided to join the other sisters who were already asleep. Helen and Gertrude snore away, while Elizabeth's arm dangled over the side of the bed.

Meanwhile, in the ship pilot's house, the navigator in his early 30s looked out over the ship's stern through the port. Near him, the ship's steward in his 20s guided the ship by the binnacle. Suddenly, the phone on the wall rang.

The navigator answered. "Yes?"

The engineer in his 40s at the boiler room communicated with him. "Sir. There is a problem."

"What kind of problem?"

"One of the engines is losing power fast."

"Why?"

"A boiler is going to be down."

"Down?"

"I-I, Sir. We are trying to repair it now. But we don't know if we can fix it. At the present rate, she can only hit 3 knots. But no more."

"Well, you're the engineer! Fix the damn problem."

"We might have to dock for some badly needed parts."

The navigator was lost in thought.

"Sir. Are you there?"

"Yes. I heard you…I'll alert the captain."

"I, Sir."

They end the call.

The steward turned to the navigator with a worried look. "Problem, Sir?"

Disgust came over him. "Looks like one of the boilers might blow."

"That's all we need."

Navigator picked up the hand receiver and began to crack the phone.

"That will not be necessary, sir."

"Pardon me, Steward?"

"I saw the captain making his rounds on the deck not too long ago, sir."

The navigator hung up the receiver again and left.

Later that night, in the ship's boiler room, the captain, in his 50s, the executive officer, who appeared to be in his early 40s, the navigator, the engineer, and the engineer's young assistant in his 20s stood by the inoperable boiler. Dread painted their faces.

The captain addressed the engineer as he stared at the boiler. "How much coal will she burn?"

"Oh. I would say about 3 tons, Captain. No more."

"Hmm. It looks like it's certainly going to delay our destination."

The executive officer chimed in. "And you say the second boiler is not much better?"

"Right, sir. The rotary stoker looks like it might go out at any moment."

The executive officer shook his head. "We should have overhauled the boilers in

Southampton when we had the chance."

Captain nodded. "Yes. But that would have taken at least weeks, and besides, the Red Cross is in tight capital these days." He took a deep breath as he pondered momentarily. He sternly looks at the boilers and turns to his navigator. "Telegraph the Red Cross. Tell them of our situation. We might have to dock soon for badly needed repairs. See if they can send a charter to take the passengers to Durban." He thought for a moment. "If I'm correct. We are just a day's sail from Walvis Bay."

The executive officer appeared confused. "Walvis Bay?"

"Yes," Captain said with a reassuring smile. "It's in the German South West Africa region. We will dock there." The captain turned to the navigator. "What are you waiting for?"

"Yes, Sir." Navigator quickly left the boiler room.

"I will inform the passengers tomorrow after they have consumed their breakfast. I don't want to spoil their appetite."

Everyone nodded in agreement.

The following morning, the wardroom mess section was filled with chatter as everyone was finishing their breakfast. The captain walked in with his executive officer close behind. They both stopped at the tables. Silence fell over the room as everyone turned to look at him. It was as if everyone knew he had something important to say.

"I hope everyone has experienced an enjoyable voyage so far. The weather will be pleasant today. And it appears everyone has consumed a wonderful breakfast." The captain cleared his throat. His demeanor became serious. "Unfortunately, that is not all. I have some news. News, I dare say, you will find disheartening. One of our boilers has gone down. As a result, the engines will not have enough power to sail to our final destination."

Shock and anger registered on the faces of the passengers. Dorothy shook her head in disbelief.

Pierre stood up. "What do you mean the boiler is down, Captain? Was not this vessel inspected before setting sail?"

"To my knowledge, she was."

A male passenger in his 50s stood. "What do you mean by your knowledge? Was she checked or not?"

"I assure you; we took every precaution before we departed."

Pierre waved his arms. "This is unbelievable!"

Martha voiced her concern. "So, my dear Captain, what is the alternative?"

"I have telegraphed the Red Cross, informing them of our situation. We will dock the following day at Walvis Bay for badly needed repairs. I shall also inquire about obtaining a charter to Durban."

CHAPTER 4 – SAIL AWAY

Mutterings fill the room once more. Diana looked around apprehensively.

A British officer serving as a physician stood. "What happens if there is no bloody charter?"

"Then the only thing we can do is sit and wait. The repairs will take several weeks. Then, the Princess of Wales can depart from Walvis Bay."

"Several weeks?" Pierre said.

"Yes. We are projecting several weeks to gather all the necessary parts and repair her properly." The captain smiled at everyone, trying to bring some comfort in an otherwise gloomy situation. "Now, my executive officer will fill you in on what accommodations are available once we reach the Bay." The captain exited as rumblings were heard among the passengers.

The hospital ship docked at Walvis Bay that day. Fifty or so passengers left the ship for a leisurely walk. The vessel remained at port until repairs were to be completed. Walvis Bay was a British colony in the Cape, while the surrounding region was German South West Africa. This region was a colony of the German Empire from 1884 until 1915. The Germans were drawn into this land by the economic possibilities of diamond and copper mining. It bordered Angola in the north and British Bechuanaland to the east.

The nuns stood near the ramp, engaged in a

heated discussion, dressed in their habits, as Diana stated her viewpoint about traveling by land: "...You heard the captain. There might not be a charter!"

Dorothy replied, "That hardly matters, Sister Diana. We will not help the wounded if we don't make it to Pretoria alive! We hardly know anything about this land!"

Helen was equally not supported by Diana's willingness to travel to their destination alone. "There is no way I will travel across the hot, humid desert. I'll wait out here like everyone else."

Gertrude addressed Diana. "How far is it to Pretoria?"

"About nine hundred miles. More or less."

Helen lets out a sarcastic laugh. "Nine hundred miles! Now I know the Sister is insane."

"The captain said it will be several weeks until we arrive at Durban, and then another week before we arrive in Pretoria by train. Provided the Boer forces have not destroyed all the bridges and tracks. Don't you see? We may never make it if we don't leave now."

The sisters noticed a German dock worker in his 50s who was loading a box on a freight wagon.

Dorothy addressed him. "Excuse me, Sir. Is there a train station nearby?

He communicated in his heavy German accent as he continued to load the wagon. "It's on Donkin Street by the harbor. Not far from here."

"Good. We need to travel to Pretoria as soon as

possible."

The dock worker stopped loading and looked at her in bewilderment. "Pretoria?"

"Why, Yes. We have important work to do there."

Gertrude echoed the sentiment. "Yes, we do."

"You cannot travel to Pretoria from here".

Helen rested her hands on her hips. "And why not?"

"There's a war going on, and the Boers have cut all lines to the South African Republic."

Elizabeth raised her eyebrows. "Oh dear."

"You would have to take a train to Mafikeng. From there, you can go by wagon, which will take you to Krugersdorp. It is a full ride by wagon, around 255 km, or 159 miles, for you English nuns. But the train to Mafikeng is now used by the British military."

Elizebeth smiled, "We're Irish nuns."

He replied with a non-understanding glare.

Dorothy asked, "How far to Mafikeng?"

He replied with a smile, exposing his missing central incisor teeth. "Oh, about 1,630 km."

The sisters, except for Diana, look at each other, trying to understand the distance.

"He means 1,000 miles."

Dorothy nodded, "Well, thank you, Sister Diana. And to you, as well, sir."

The German worker nodded at them and continued working as the nuns walked away.

"We'll wait and sail to Port Durban and receive

safe passage to Pretoria as planned."

"But with a good guide, Sister Helen, we can reach Pretoria in the same amount of time, if not sooner."

"Oh? You are well-versed in desert travels, Sister Diana? I dare say I shouldn't be surprised since you appear to have the lust for wandering."

Diana gave Helen an angry look.

Dorothy had enough. "Settle down, both of you! We represent the sisterhood, and I intend to leave a good impression."

Adeline glanced at the sun. "Me and the hot sun do not always agree, Sister Diana."

Elizabeth lets out a giggle. "I think the travel will be lovely."

Helen was not amused. "No one is conversing with you, Sister Elizabeth!"

Dorothy took a deep breath. "I wish there was another way."

Adeline added, "I will admit. Staying here until we arrive at Durban can be quite boring indeed."

"It beats traveling nine hundred miles in no man's land, Sister Adeline."

"Now, Sister Helen," Diana explained. "You must put your faith in the Lord."

"Only if we are not stupid, Sister Diana. And traveling through the hot desert is stupidity at its best."

An uneasy silence fell over the group.

Diana continued with her point. "We can reach Pretoria with a guide."

Dorothy rolled her eyes. "Sister Diana, with all due respect. Traveling to Pretoria is no easy task, even with a guide. How about the mode of transportation? I don't think Sister Gertrude is up to the task."

"Oh! Don't let my age scare you, Sisters."

"It will not all be desert," Diana replied.

Dorothy took another deep breath, regarding the situation. Elizabeth suddenly let out a laugh. Helen turned to her with a stern look.

"What are you laughing about now?"

"This is such a fun trip."

Helen shook her head in disgust.

Dorothy seemed to consider it. "And where might we find one of these guides?"

Dorothy's remark enraged Helen further. "Sister Dorothy!"

Diana suddenly saw a group of camels being led by three African men. She smiled." The Lord has already found us our guides."

The others followed her gaze.

Several hours later, on the outskirts of Walvis Bay, one can witness dunes of every magnitude everywhere. The nuns in their habits were accompanied by three African guides: Jabavu, mid-40s; Tiyo, 20s; and Adam, mid-30s. Adam was the only guide who spoke any English. All three were from the Hottentot tribe and appeared fit and trim.

Diana, Dorothy, and Adeline sat on camels. Tiyo

was helping Gertrude mount her camel. Jabavu struggled to get Elizabeth to sit on her camel. She placed one foot on the stirrup and slowly pulled the other leg over the saddle. However, her heavy body weight almost caused her to fall over as she leaned too far onto the other side. Elizabeth cried out for help as she could not pull herself back up. Jabavu was losing his grip on her as she continued to lean over to the other side. Adam quickly came to Jabavu's aid, ran over to Elizabeth, and held her in place with great effort. Jabavu began to pull Elizabeth up as he continued to grab her leg. Adam also pushed up, and slowly but surely, Elizabeth finally sat in the proper position on top of the camel. Diana, Dorothy, and Adeline were relieved to see Elizabeth sitting upright on the camel.

A concerned look came over Dorothy. "Are you all right?"

Elizabeth giggled in delight. "Oh my! That was fun. I enjoy myself."

Dorothy took a deep breath. Tiyo had Gertrude mounted on her camel with not much difficulty. She looked around, surprised. "I suddenly feel so high. Like I'm on another plateau."

Adeline managed to smile. "It's a shame we don't have camels back home."

Everyone was ready to depart except for Helen, who defiantly sat on the ground. The others turn to her.

"I won't do it. I simply won't. There is no way I'm getting on that stupid, dumb camel."

Diana tried reasoning with her. "Sister Helen, one cannot trek through the Namib Desert on foot. You must get on the camel if we are to go through the Namib Desert."

Adam smiled, encouraging Helen. "Truth be told, the camel you will be riding on is called a dromedary and quite an extraordinary animal. She can travel about 100 miles a day and run up to 25 miles per hour. Unless racing, which they can go even faster."

Helen seemed unimpressed. Adam turned to Dorothy. She nodded at him. The three guides then approached Helen.

Dread came over Helen's face. "What is going on here?"

Dorothy was losing her patience. "It's time to go, Sister Helen. We want to cover as much ground as we can today."

Suddenly, the guides picked Helen off the ground and carried her to the assigned camel.

Helen struggled, waving her arms and kicking her legs. "Put me down this instant. I'm not a piece of luggage you can do as you please."

All the other nuns giggled at the sight of Helen's protests.

"I swear by almighty God! Mother Superior will hear about this. You wait and see."

But the nuns continued to find the event humorous, as their giggles turned into laughter. Helen hit Jabavu and Tiyo with closed fists as they lifted her on the camel. Sitting upright on the camel, everyone was quiet, as all eyes were on Helen. Helen said nothing as her face turned red with rage. She was dumbfounded at the whole dreadful event.

Dusk had begun to settle as everyone was finally on their camels, leaving Walvis Bay's outskirts. They decided to stop to check if everything was in place. Adam was to lead the way with Jabavu. Bringing up the rear was Tiyo. He held a rope attached to six Bactrian camels hauling the nun's luggage, water, food provisions purchased in Walvis Bay, and several Mauser 7mm Rifles. To their immediate east lies the Namib Desert. Dorothy turned to Adam.

"Is it necessary to bring along firearms?"

"Yes, Sister. We have a way to go, and there was no telling what we might encounter."

Adeline interjected. "Like lions and tigers!"

Adam smiled back at Adeline. "In the dunes, no. But further away, anything is possible."

Elizabeth expressed a worried look on her face. "Can we be eaten?"

Adam smiled, "Don't worry, Sister."

The nun's worries began to annoy Dorothy. "Enough nonsense! Everything will be just fine. The Lord is watching over us."

Gertrude's reassuring smile. "Amen."

The other nuns nodded their heads in agreement.

Satisfied, Dorothy commanded. "Whenever

you are ready, Adam."

"Yes, Sister."

Adam said something to Jabavu in their native tongue. Jabavu quickly replied and nodded his head. Satisfied, Adam began to proceed, and everyone else slowly moved. However, Helen's camel did not move. It just stood there. Jabavu struck the camel in the buttocks with a stick in his hand. Helen's camel began to make progress.

Gertrude gasped. "This is so uplifting!"

"I feel like an Arab sheik." Elizabeth bellowed.

Diana and Adeline laughed at their remarks as Dorothy smiled.

CHAPTER 5 – THE TREK

Several days had passed, and this day, like the others, was hot and dry in the Namib Desert in German South West Africa. The caravan continued to make its way through the vast dunes. The heat was starting to take its toll on the nuns, who were compensating for it by modifying their habits. Some nuns had their sleeves rolled up, while others had skirts to their thighs, such as Diana and Adeline, who looked especially attractive in this fashion as they rode close behind Dorothy and Adam, who were leading the group. Helen was behind Dorothy and Adeline and looked somewhat fatigued, as she continuously wiped her forehead with a small towel. The rest of the caravan was behind Helen.

Dorothy turned toward Adam. "You're certain there is more than just dunes ahead of us?"

"Oh yes, Sister. But for the first several days or so, we will see nothing but dunes."

Gertrude wiped her brow with a handkerchief. "This is going to be a long journey on these camels."

"Don't worry, Sister. You will not always be riding."

"I do not understand?"

"Eventually, we will travel down the Orange

CHAPTER 5 – THE TREK

River and into the Vaal. It should take us to the station at Vereeniging. Where my family's from"

Dorothy replied, "Well, that's a relief."

Gertrude echoes the sentiment. "It sure is."

Dorothy changed the subject. "Do you miss your family in Vereeniging?"

"Yes, I do, Sister."

"Well, the Sisters are glad to have found you and your friends on short notice."

Adam replied with a grateful smile.

"Tell me, how is your English so good?"

"My parents were servants to a German family in Luderitz. The family insisted that my parents speak both German and English. My mother spoke English well, while my father preferred German."

Diana joined in. "And I suppose Adam, you took after your Mom?"

"Yes, I did."

Dorothy continued, "What do you think about the fighting?"

"I don't know much about it, Sister. But I believe it will end soon."

"May I ask why?"

"The Boers are no match for the British Empire."

"But the Boer won the first war."

"Yes, Sister. But the British gave up without any true struggle. I believe this time the British are serious."

"Why is that?"

"Gold."

"It appears everyone wants gold. But gold, like all other forms of money, will only lead to disaster."

Meanwhile, Elizabeth rode alone beside Gertrude, with Jabavu close behind. Tiyo was behind, holding the rope and guiding the supply camels. Suddenly, Elizabeth spotted a lonely black-backed jackal wandering a short distance away.

"Oh. That's a-a-a..."

Jabavu said something in his language, but Elizabeth did not understand.

Gertrude points at it. "I think it's a jackal, Sister Elizabeth."

"Jackal?"

"That's the name of the animal."

"Oh! Silly me. I should have known."

Elizabeth turned and smiled with embarrassment at Jabavu. He returned it with a broad smile, displaying his perfect white teeth.

"My, you have such pretty teeth."

Jabavu replied with another grin.

Meanwhile, Helen displayed a dreadful frown. She murmurs as if talking to herself." I hate the sand. I hate the heat. And I hate this place."

The following day, the caravan continued its journey through the sandy dunes in the Namib Desert in German South West Africa. They could see several dust devils kicking up over the horizon, as the gust from the sand started to pick up. But they continued their journey on the camels as best they could, shielding their faces from the sand.

The caravan decided it would be best to stop and set up another camp. As the nuns traveled through the sand dunes, they began to see some plant life and a few trees—everyone except for Tiyo erected tents for the night.

Tiyo was a very short distance away. He retrieved some vegetation from the sandy ground using his pocket knife. The vegetation took the shape of green-like balls with thorny skin. Using his knife, Tiyo carefully peels open the green balls. Diana walked over to Tiyo and noticed him eating the vegetation. Tiyo turned and smiled at Diana as he chewed. He offered her a sample, but she politely refused. Suddenly, Adam approached Diana and Tiyo. Tiyo immediately offered Adam some nourishment using his blade. Adam slid the food into his mouth. He began to chew on it as Diana looked on curiously. He offered some to her. But again, she politely refused.

"What is it?"

"It's a Nara Melon. They are quite good. It is a staple food among my people. You should try it. Here. "

Tiyo handed Diana a piece. She took a cautious bite.

"Hmmm. It tastes a little bitter. But it's not bad at all."

Tiyo gathered more melons, using his knife again to cut through the stems. He continued to eat them, and Adam did the same with his knife, as

Diana smiled at them.

That night at the campsite, the guides had managed to build a fire in front of the tents. As in previous nights in the camp sites, Dorothy and the rest of the nuns removed their habits and wore something more casual after finishing their travels for the day. It was the only time the guides had the opportunity to see the nuns without their habits on.

Before they slept, Gertrude usually cooked some dry meat and potatoes, while Dorothy made fresh tea from the few cooking utensils they gathered. The remaining nuns sat comfortably around the fire. Some talked, while others sang. Adam carefully observed the fire.

Jabavu and Tiyo stood watch a short distance away. They would glance up at the night sky, holding their Mauser rifles.

The guides felt it would be less taxing if they rested and camped during the day, and traveled at night from that day forward, due to heat exhaustion, until they reached Cape Colony. This would conserve water. The nuns did not like the idea of traveling at night. Afraid of any wildlife that might be roaming the desert. However, Adam assured them that it would be safe. The moonlight or the bright stars would offer sufficient light, and the guides will be ready to use their firearms if needed. The nuns reluctantly agreed. Traveling at night, they looked up and saw numerous stars gazing down at them, as if the stars were speaking to them.

A week later, the nuns were in Cape Colony in South Africa. At the time, the Colony was under British rule. It was once under Dutch authority until it was transferred to the British after the Battle of Blaauwberg, which led to the Anglo-Dutch Treaty in 1814.

As night approached, the nuns managed to set up their tents. As usual, they sat comfortably in their casual clothes around the campfire while the guides stood watch after everyone had eaten.

Meanwhile, Diana lay on top of a blanket beside one of the tents; a small kerosene lamp served as her light. She wrote a letter she planned to mail to Sister Catherine once the nuns reached Pretoria, summarizing their process.

"Our trip, Sister Catherine, is going as expected. But there is so much to see. So much. I was told by Adam that the sand dunes are the tallest in the world. How he knows this, I don't know. But the guides are so knowledgeable and so caring. We promise to pay them when we reach the destination of Vereeniging. From there, we Sisters shall board a train to Pretoria. But as I write now, everything is so peaceful. So beautiful and so still. You look at the heavens above, and the stars seem so close. It's as if you can almost touch them. But I must not be lost in this beauty forever. For I know there is still so much to be done..."

As Diana wrote, she looked up and saw that the

night sky was full of stars. Many constellations were visible and appeared almost within reach.

Diana recalled her wonderful time on Fish River Canyon in German South West Africa.

"...Soon we reached the Fish Grand Canyon, where the Fish River flows into. Adam, the only
guide who can speak English perfectly, I might add, says the canyon is the second largest one, next to the one in America. How he knows this, I don't know. But he says the canyon presents a dramatic assortment of colors. It's a canyon within a canyon."

Writing the passage reminded her of the caravan, standing close to the edge, looking down at the River Canyon, except for Helen. She sat close behind on the large rock, appearing downcast. The majesty of the canyon, with its high cliffs and various terrain, can be observed from the cliffs. The Fish River runs slowly through it. The deep canyon stretches aimlessly, as the end is nowhere in sight.

The nuns made it to Augrabies Falls in the Cape Colony. Diana wrote:

"... And from the canyon, we came across the Augrabies Falls. Here, the Orange River divides German South West Africa from the rest of South Africa, surges across a rocky terrain, and plunges into a deep ravine. The Bushmen tribe named the Falls the Augrabies, a place of great noise. I wish

you Sisters could be here to see this beauty."

Diana reflected on the Augrabies Falls, where the nuns passed through. The caravan stood across the falls as the nuns looked at it. Everyone except Helen appeared in awe at this mighty water surge plummeting several hundred feet to the depths below. Helen displayed no enthusiasm over the wondrous sight as she continually yawned.

The nuns continued their trek through Cape Colony.

"... It's so inspiring. Seeing God's hand at work. Knowing that everything here and above has a purpose. Knowing the splendor and beauty of Africa. Which I will never see again. But do not worry, my letter will keep you updated on what you are missing...Love Sister Diana."

As she wrote her final passage, she recalled the caravan on their camels traveling along their route. Trees were more plentiful. However, the ground still appeared sandy in the Kalahari Basin. Overhead, a beautiful rainbow arched against a rustically colored sky with small amounts of rain overhead. But the caravan continued on its journey as if following the rainbow.

Several days later, the nuns wearing their habits and guides sailed down the Orange River in Cape Colony on a 40-foot steamer boat, complete with one vertical boiler and a connecting engine near the bow area, as they could hear the engine clanking alone. There was a portable canopy providing shade for a portion of the stern area, and a woodpile next to the boiler to be used as a fuel source. The boat was wide enough to accommodate all nine passengers. Tiyo was at the tiller, steering the boat at the stern. All the nuns stood on the boat looking out towards the banks of the mighty river, except for Helen, who was sitting and preoccupied with reading a novel of some sort. The nuns secured the boat from a local trader for a rental fee. The small steamer was to take them to Vereeniging. The nuns pooled some money and gave it to Adam to secure the vessel, provided it was worthy.

The nuns saw several elephants traveling together from the port side, with the mother leading the way. Her calves followed close behind. The mother saw the boat and raised her trunk. She gave a loud, shrill cry. The nuns raised their hands and waved at the mother as a sign of greeting. Diana put her hands together around her mouth and yelled in return. But her sounds were no match from the mother elephant.

Several chacma baboons ran along the bank on the starboard side as if following the boat. Gertrude and Adeline gave them a humorous look. The boiler lets out a small tail of smoke as Adam puts more wood in the boiler. Dorothy decided to approach him as Jabavu looked over the bow with a Mauser rifle in his hand. Adam noticed that Dorothy was approaching, so he stood and moved over to her.

"Be careful, Sister. I don't want to see you burn yourself."

"Thank you, Adam. You will have to show me how to operate this vessel."

"Certainly, Sister. I will let you know when we will need more wood."

"Fine. Then we shall stop."

"Yes, Sister."

Diana approached. "This river is so serene."

"Don't let the river fool you, Sister."

"What do you mean?"

"This mighty river can be rough sometimes, especially when we hit white water."

"White water?"

Dorothy was quick with an answer. "He means the rapids, Sister Diana. But don't you worry. This boat will do just fine. Does this vessel have a name?"

"Not that I know of, Sister."

Diana smiles. "Let's call it the Ship of Hope."

Elizabeth approached with an alarmed expression as she pointed towards the riverbanks just ahead of the bow.

"Look!"

Several large hippopotamuses were on the bank and then went into the river. Jabavu raised his rifle at them as they neared the boat. Adam addressed Jabavu in his native tongue. Jabavu then decided to rest his rifle on Adam's command.

"The hippopotamuses are no threat to us, Sisters, as long as you stay in the boat. Besides, there are only a few left."

Elizabeth lets out a sigh of relief.

Dorothy replied. "Why is this, Adam?"

"They were once common in South Africa but have since been slaughtered for their meat and hides. Even their teeth are used for one's teeth wear because of their fine-grained ivory."

Adam addressed Jabavu in their native tongue. Jabavu replied with a wide grin, displaying his bright white teeth.

Dorothy's eyes widen. "So that explains it."

Elizabeth beamed. "My, I wish I had teeth like that."

Dorothy shook her head. "Sister Elizabeth! You would want dentals from hippopotamuses?"

Sounding embarrassed. "Sorry, Sister."

Gertrude came with a small burner heated by kerosene fuel. Who wants tea?"

Elizabeth grinned. "I'll take some."

Adeline joined it. "Me too."

Dorothy agreed. "Yes. A spot of tea sounds good."

A week passed, and the boat was finally on the Vaal River, bordering the Orange Free State. The name Vaal is a Dutch name meaning dull because the waters on the river appeared to give it a dull, muddy look during the flood seasons. Above the river, a full moon was bearing its light down on the quiet river below.

CHAPTER 5 – THE TREK

Everyone appeared preoccupied as Dorothy, Adeline, and Elizabeth sat alone at a small table and read their Bibles. A kerosene lamp provided some additional light. Gertrude sat on a bench, attending to her knitting while Helen sat across from her and read her novel with great interest. Jabavu guided the boat with the tiller while Adam sat next to him. Adam was reviewing a map as another kerosene lamp provided some further light.

Meanwhile, Tiyo stood on the bow with his rifle. Diana was preoccupied with the river as she stood overlooking the water. A slight breeze caused her habit to ripple in the wind. Her beauty matched the moonlight shining down on the river, giving it a glowing look. Suddenly, she looked above and noticed a star falling across the night sky. She smiled as she talked to herself.

"This is truly God's country." She turned and decided to walk over to Adam and Jabavu. Adam looked up at Diana.

"One day you must let me steer the Hope."
"Yes, Sister."

Diana gave Adam a beautiful smile as her eyes sparkled.

"Where are you from, Sister?"
"Limerick."
"Limerick?"
"Yes. Ireland."

"I have never had the pleasure of visiting Europe."

"You must come and visit us one day when this war is over."

"I will, Sister. I will."

"So, Captain. How long before we reach Vereeniging?"

"I think we shall reach our destination on the third day, Sister." Adam momentarily looked at the moonlight and turned to Diana. "Your country. Do you miss it much?"

"Yes, as all the sisters here do."

Adam nodded.

"I miss my family, Adam. I haven't seen them in quite some time. You said you have a family in Vereeniging?"

"Yes. I have two older brothers."

"What do they do?"

"They work for a mining company."

"I imagine they will be thrilled to see you."

"Oh yes, Sister, indeed."

Diana smiled at Adam. He returned it.

The following day, it was decided to anchor the boat off an embankment in the Vaal River for some more wood. The nuns were wearing other clothing attire, as Gertrude and Elizabeth were washing their habits from the side of the boat.

By the vessel, Diana, Adeline, Jabavu, and Tiyo

cut small branches of wood from trees using machetes.

Dorothy and Adam held a discussion on the boat as Helen sat near the bow, reading her novel. Unexpectedly, everyone heard artillery fire from a distance. Everyone stopped their activity as they stared toward the sounding guns, except for Helen. Her eyes were still on the novel.

Gertrude sounded alarmed. "What was that?"

Helen replied calmly, her eyes on the novel. "Cannon fire. What did you think?"

"Cannon fire?" Elizabeth exclaimed.

Helen with her usual sarcasm. "There is a war going on. Is there not?"

Gertrude injected. "But it sounds so close."

The artillery sounded again.

Adam looked out in the distance. "There must be some fighting near Klerksdorp."

"We will reach Vereeniging soon?" Dorothy asked.

"Yes, Sister."

Adam turned to Jabavu and Tiyo and commanded them to stop cutting using their native language. Jabavu and Tiyo laid their blades down and gathered the small branches on the ground.

"That's enough wood for now, Sisters."

Diana and Adeline, in turn, stopped their cutting.

"That's it?"

"Yes, Sister Adeline," Diana replied. "We have plenty of wood now."

Dorothy echoed her remarks. "Yes. It's time to head back to the boat."

Adeline disagreed with Dorothy. "Are you sure?"

"Sorry, Sister Woodsman. But I don't like the sounds of those guns."

"Rats!"

Dorothy then turned to Gertrude and Elizabeth. "I believe you two have done enough washing."

Gertrude and Elizabeth show no sign of arguing as they gather the wet clothes. Dorothy turned to Helen, who continued to read her novel. Dorothy shook her head disapprovingly at Helen but decided to say nothing. Adam checked the small-cylinder engine before starting the boat again.

As promised, the nuns arrived at the train station in Vereeniging several days later. The railroad station was crowded as various people boarded a train to Pretoria. The nuns stood at the passenger platform. They were dressed in their black habits and holding some of their luggage. Standing next to them were Adam, Jabavu, and Tiyo. The nuns said their goodbyes to the guides before boarding the train. They had melancholy written all over their faces. Gertrude and Elizabeth began to shed a few tears. Helen, on the other hand, displayed a look of indifference. Dorothy handed Adam an envelope. He opened it and saw currency in British Pounds. He thumbed over the currency, and a smile appeared on his face.

"Thank you, Sister."

"I believe that should be sufficient to compensate for your services. "

"Yes, Sister, it does."

Dorothy gave them a warm smile. "We shall miss you all. I know we would not have reached our destination without your help."

Diana echoed her sentiments. "Yes. Your service was invaluable."

"I didn't think we would make it this far," Adeline said.

"You must have faith, Sister."

The nuns laugh momentarily at Adam's comments, except for Helen.

"I believe that is something we nuns should already know." Dorothy reminded them.

Gertrude wiped a tear from her eye using a handkerchief. "Yes. This is true."

The train's whistle blew.

Dorothy commended. "Well, Sisters, it's time to depart."

With tears welling in her eyes, Elizabeth hugged all three guides. "I know we already hugged, but I will miss you all."

All three guides returned the hugs with happy smiles. Dorothy boarded the train first. The others followed behind; each turned to say goodbye to their guides. The guides, in turn, wave their goodbyes. Helen, the last to enter, turned toward the guides. Her uncaring expression suddenly turned into a happy and caring smile. The guides likewise return with a smile as they wave to her. Helen then entered the train. The train immediately began its final destination to Pretoria as its whistle blew.

With all their foot traveling, the nuns fell fast asleep in their seats. Helen and Gertrude snored away as the train traveled toward Pretoria in the South African Republic.

A slightly tall man in his mid-30s walked toward the nuns as he went to his seat. His name was Juan Sanchez. Besides appearing handsome, he was a licensed doctor from Spain who volunteered to aid the Red Cross in the war. He stopped and noticed something on the floor. A closer look revealed a rosary lying by the feet of Elizabeth, who sat across from Diana. Juan decided to walk up to Elizabeth and retrieve the rosary. Diana suddenly opened her eyes and stared at Juan. His charming looks took her by surprise. From his kneeling position, Juan looked up as he held the rosary. His eyes meet Diana's. They both stare at each other in total silence. They both appear to be taken by each other. Suddenly, Juan spoke to her softly.

"Do you know who this belongs to?"

Diana closed her eyes as she pretended to go back to sleep. Juan looked at her and noticed how beautiful she was. He smiled at her with the rosary in hand. He decided to leave the rosary on Elizabeth's lap. He stood and went back to his seat. Diana opened her eyes and turned, as her eyes followed Juan to his seat. He reached for his seat to sit, and unexpectedly turned toward the direction of Diana. Diana quickly turned and closed her eyes again to avoid being noticed. Juan observed her apparently asleep and decided to rest his head back to get some sleep. Diana opened her eyes and gazed at him. She then closed her eyes again as a small smile danced on her lips.

CHAPTER 6 – A NEW BEGINNING

Several hours later, the train reached the Pretoria train station after stopping in Johannesburg. The weather was clear, and the station was filled with people as they walked about to meet arriving visitors.

Passengers exited the train, some carrying their luggage. The nuns also exited the train. They appeared to be in merry spirits.

"Thank God, we're finally here."

Elizabeth exited behind Helen as she stepped onto the passenger platform. "Oh, our trip was wonderful."

Helen, without looking at her. "Pipe down. You don't want to spoil my good mood."

Elizabeth reacted with a grin. Meanwhile, Diana, Dorothy, and Adeline walked toward the train station gate.

Nearby, Diana spotted Juan walking to the baggage room. She stopped, her gaze lingering on him. Adeline noticed.

"What's wrong?"

Diana did not reply as she continued to stare at Juan.

"Sister Diana?"

"Oh. I was thinking about something."

"And what might that have been, may I ask?"

Diana smiled at her. "I shall never tell."

Diana and Adeline began to giggle. Gertrude, Helen, and Elizabeth reached Diana and Adeline.

"What are you hyenas galvanizing about?"

Adeline replied, "Oh, it's nothing, Sister Helen."

"Figures."

Helen walked past them, with Gertrude close behind.

Elizebeth was all smiles. "Not to worry. She is in her good mood."

Diana and Adeline smiled at Elizabeth as the three continued to walk toward the gate.

Pretoria was the capital of the South African Republic during the war. Buildings, including the capital building, line the main avenue. Various pedestrians walk about, while others travel in horse carriages.

A small group of Boer soldiers moved about. Most rode on horseback and carried rifles. They wore rough farming clothes and wide-brimmed hats. Many had slung belts of bullets over both shoulders.

The nuns were shown to their boarding house, which was near Volks Hospital, also known as Volkshospitaal, a Boer medical facility, where they were assigned to. The boarding house itself was basic. It had the essential elements. Each room had two beds. There were also two plain dresser drawers with mirrors and two portable closets. Down the hall was a restroom area with several showers for the nuns to share. There was also a kitchen with a wood-burning stove, icebox, sink, and cabinets. Elizabeth was selected to be Diana's roommate.

The following morning, after the nuns had breakfast at the boarding house, they arrived at the hospital. They were dressed in their habits, with a band on their left arm denoting the Red Cross symbol. They walked past a row of bedridden patients in the patient ward. They were a combination of injured Boer commandoes and civilians. Most of the patients were asleep. Ruth, who was in her 50s, was the head nurse and gave the nuns a brief tour of the hospital on their first day of duty.

"As you can see, most of our beds are occupied. Let me assure you, we run a tight ship here. We have staff nurses who make hourly rounds."

Adeline raised her hand.

"Yes, Sister...?"

"Adeline."

"I'm sorry, Adeline. I didn't catch your name earlier."

"How many of these patients are from the war?"

"At this point, only half. But as the war continues, we expect this to increase dramatically.

CHAPTER 6 – A NEW BEGINNING

Normally, the wounded are first treated at the field and then sent here for full recovery. But they are starting to be overwhelmed and are now bringing some of the wounded directly to us. That is, those that can make it."

Dorothy was next with her question. "You mentioned most of the beds are occupied. If so, where will the incoming go?"

"An adjacent ward, as well as large auxiliary tents, are being added. Once completed, they should house an extra 200 beds for the wounded."

"I see."

"Of course, we don't know when the next batch of wounded will arrive."

Elizabeth had a question. "So not all the wounded are treated in the auxiliary hospitals at the battlefields?"

"Like I said, they can get quite too busy. Besides, the field units miss a thing or two. Or they are so rushed with the incoming wounded that they have us do it."

Helen turned to Elizabeth. "Aren't you listening?"

"Just put a temporary bandage, and then ship the wounded here." Gertrude said.

"Exactly, Gertrude." Ruth stopped as she came across a patient named Paul. He was in his 30s. Ruth went over and retrieved his chart hanging on the bedpost. She quickly observed it while the nuns stood around the bed. She addressed him while her eyes were on the chart. "How do you feel today, Paul?"

"Fine, ma'am. Are the nuns here to visit? Huh?"

Ruth hung the chart back on the bedpost, satisfied with what she read. "No. They're here to work."

"Work?"

Dorothy interjected. "That's right. We came from Ireland to help the wounded."

"Ireland! You don't say."

The nuns giggled.

"Paul suffered a bullet wound in his Gastrocnemius."

Elizabeth looked confused. "Gastrocnemius?"

Diana, with her training background, was quick with the answer. "His calf muscle."

Ruth smiled at Diana. "Yes."

Gertrude addressed Paul. "So, how is the fighting going?"

"We have the British running. They think they can beat us. I say, just wait and see."

"Paul was wounded near Magersfontein. A hundred casualties have been reported from there."

Adeline raised her eyebrows. "A hundred casualties! How dreadful."

"Only a few died. The rest were just cut up and wounded. Like me, for instance." He then looked up at Ruth. "Isn't that right, ma'am?"

"Yes, Paul."

Dorothy posed a question. "When will Paul be released?"

"According to his charts, he should be released early next week."

Paul addressed the nuns with a smile, as he became fixated on Diana." I didn't know there were such pretty sisters."

Diana smiled back at Paul.

Helen's nostrils flared, and her mouth tightened. "Scoundrel! Do you not know who you are addressing?"

"I mean no disrespect."

Diana gave him a warm smile. "Oh, that's quite all right, Paul."

"Be a good lad, Paul."

"Yes, Ruth… I mean, yes, ma'am."

Ruth headed off to survey the other bedridden patients. The nuns follow close behind.

"Luckily, there have only been minor losses to the British so far. But I fear that will change soon."

Dorothy narrowed her eyes. "Oh?"

"The British are sending waves of reinforcements from their Commonwealth nations. Like nearby Australia, India, and New Zealand."

"How many?" Dorothy asked.

"The last I heard, a hundred thousand soldiers

will arrive within the next few weeks."

Gertrude's jaws drop open. "My. The British are serious. Aren't they?"

"They don't want to repeat the same mistakes they made in the first war."

Suddenly, Ruth stopped to look at another patient's chart on the bedpost. The patient, however, was asleep, and the other nuns gathered around the bed.

A short distance away, Juan walked over to a patient's bed wearing a white doctor's coat. A nurse accompanied him. He started to converse with the male patient. Diana turned and noticed Juan. She was surprised to see him again. However, Juan did not notice the nuns as he continued to talk with the patient. Ruth finished her examination of the chart. She proceeded to walk away as she continued her tour of the patients. Diana addressed Ruth.

"Beg pardon, Ruth?"

She stopped and turned toward Diana. "Yes, Diana."

"Who is that gentleman examining that patient over there?"

Diana looked in Juan's direction. Ruth followed Diana's gaze and saw Juan conversing with the patient. Ruth turned toward Diana.

"Oh. That's Doctor Juan Sanchez."

"Doctor?"

"Why yes. He is a resident physician on this ward.

Elizabeth with a beaming smile. "My, he's handsome."

Helen was not pleased. "Elizabeth! Watch your mouth. You are a representative of the church."

"Don't worry. None of you will see too much of the dashing doctor."

"Do you mean we will not be helping with the patients, Ruth?"

"You will, Dorothy, but not here. Except for Diana, everyone else will be assigned to non-medical functions due to your limited backgrounds. You will be most useful as administrative aides in these areas."

Helen could not understand. "But not Diana?"

"Diana has formal education and completed training as a medical nurse. So, I will need her here. Especially when the expected high number of wounded arrives."

Adeline nudged Diana. "Why, you lucky Sister."

Gertrude sounded disappointed. "You get to see all the action."

Ruth injected, "In this hospital, everyone has an important role to play."

The nuns looked downcast, except for Diana, who wore a smile.

Dorothy tried to cheer them up." Now, Sisters. You heard the head nurse. We are here to aid the

Red Cross where it is most needed."

Ruth continued her tour. "Come along now."

She guided them through the remaining ward, and the nuns followed her. However, Diana appeared to lag behind.

"Next, I would like to show you our..."

As Ruth continued, Diana stole another look at Juan. He walked away, leaving the patient with the nurse. Diana's dreamy smile came over her as she continued to look at Juan. She quickly gathered herself and turned to follow the rest of the nuns.

The following day, the nurses walked about at Volks Hospital as the ward was a beehive of activity. New patients arrived at the hospital. A Boer patient entered with cloth bandages wrapped around his entire head. He was shaking and moaning. A nurse tried to calm him down. He has lost his sight.

"Get it off me!" He exclaimed.

The nurse was holding him. "Please, sir! You must stay still!"

A legless patient was given a shot of morphine in the arm by a nurse to calm his nerves, as the shock of losing both his legs from an artillery shell was too much for him to bear.

"My legs! Where's my legs?"

Another patient was in bed with a cast on his left leg, resting on a gurney. He reached for his broken leg as he screamed in obvious pain. Diana, now a nurse, came quickly to his aid. Diana stood by his bed. She wore a nurse's uniform with the Red Cross armband around her left arm. However, she was sporting her white veil instead of a nurse's cap on her head. Around her neck rests a stethoscope. The patient was Barbee, who appears to be in his early 40s. She placed a thermometer in his mouth. She then carefully stared at the thermometer as Barbee stared back at her. He managed a flirtatious wink at her, but Diana did not react to his charms. She retrieved the thermometer from his mouth and attempted to read it. However, she could not determine the reading, so she flipped the thermometer several times with a quick flick of her wrist.

"So, what's my temperature, Sister?"

Diana replied as she focused on the thermometer. "Just a minute, Barbee." She smiled and placed the thermometer in a glass container with antiseptics beside his bed.

"It looks like your fever has gone down."

"Oh! Thank you, good Sister. For a moment, I thought I was going to catch something."

"Nonsense! Now, what did I tell you about calling me Sister?"

"I'm sorry, Diana. But back when I visited the convents as a lad, I called everyone Sister."

"We are not in a convent. We are in a hospital.

Now, you sleep well, and I will check on you later. Promise?"

"Promise, Diana."

Diana left. Barbee followed her with his eyes and a smile.

"If the angels in heaven look like her, I'd better start rereading the Bible."

Diana walked down the line of beds. She waved hello to a few patients before stopping at Tim, who was in his 20s. As Diana approached, he lay comfortably, with a smile on his face.

"How are you doing, Tim?"

"Fine, Sister"

She replied with a frown.

"... I mean, Diana."

"Did you receive a letter from your wife yet?"

"No."

"Give it some time. Because of this war, commerce is moving rather slowly." She checked his chart. "How are the stitches feeling?"

"It sometimes irritates me, and I feel like scratching it."

"No scratching. I will redress your wounds with peroxide later."

"When will the stitches come off?"

"I do not know."

Tim did not say anything as he looked downcast.

"I tell you what. Let's pray on it."

"Pray?"

"Why yes, pray. Now, please do not tell me, Timothy McGinley, you do not believe in prayers."

"I usually do not pray."

"Here. Give me your hands."

Tim raised his hands to her, and Diana clapped his with hers. They both closed their eyes as she began to pray.

"Dear God. I pray that Tim's wounds heal soon. That he will be there to see his wife deliver the birth of his first child. You know, Lord, Tim is not always faithful in his relationship with you. But I know he desires to be. I see it in his eyes. And I know he will rear his child when his baby is born, according to your word. And you will be so proud of him when he does. We ask this of you, dear Lord. Amen."

Diana and Tim open their eyes. Diana let go of his hands, and Tim began to shed a tear.

"Thank you, Diana. No one has ever prayed for me before."

"Do not thank me. Thank the Lord."

"Yes, Diana."

Diana walked away, passing several other beds.

Suddenly, Ruth approached her with a worried look on her face.

"Diana! We need you right away in the operating room."

"Me?"

"One of the nurses to assist Doctor Sanchez suddenly became ill."

"I'm to assist Doctor Sanchez?"

"I believe that is his name. Unless he changed it this morning. Are you up to it?"

"Yes, ma'am."

"Good. Then follow me."

Ruth hurried off. Diana followed.

A short time later, in an operating room, a surgical team of two nurses and a doctor operated on a male patient in his 30s on the table. The patient was unconscious, as he was drugged with local anesthetics. Sterile sheets covered the patient, except for the chest area, which was being operated on. The doctor was Juan, while Diana was one of the nurses assigned to him. The other nurse was Mary, in her 40s, who was holding a sponge in her hand. They were wearing surgical garments such as gowns, masks, and gloves. Next to the operating table was the instrument table, where the surgical instruments such as clamps, scissors, and scalpels lay. With the patient's chest cavity open, Juan examined a wound caused by a bullet. Diana was standing on the other side of the table, with her eyes fixed on Juan. Without taking his eyes off the patient's internal organs, he calls for her.

"Now that the bullet is out. We can close this wound. Diana, give me the number eight hemostat?"

CHAPTER 6 – A NEW BEGINNING

Diana quickly retrieved the clamp as Juan and Mary watched. Juan took the clamp from Diana's gloved hand and immediately placed it to stop the bleeding.

"Just one more blood vessel and that should do it." Juan clamped the blood vessel. "Mary, there."

With sponges in her hand, Mary wiped up a small amount of blood in and around the chest opening.

An hour had passed, and the operation was completed. Juan finished sewing the skin together. Mary helped him wrap bandages around the patient's torso, covering the incision area. Diana wheeled off the instrument table. While Mary's eyes were on the patient, Juan looked up and stared at Diana, puzzlingly.

After performing her duties for the day, Diana stood on the stairs in her nursing attire at the hospital's back entrance. She looked at the beautiful sunset.

Juan approached her. "Hello."

"I apologize for not introducing myself when I first saw you. I did not know we would be working together."

Juan, with a curious smile, asked, "When did you first notice me?"

"On the train."

"Oh yes. The train."

"Ah…" Diana was about to say something. But then smiled. "Oh, it's nothing."

"They say thoughts are the window to one's

soul."

"I always believe one's faith in God is the window to one's soul, doctor."

"I stopped attending church a long time ago."

Diana responded with a smile.

"How do you like your duties so far...Sister Diana. Or should I call you Diana?"

"Diana will do." Paused. "It's interesting. Some patients are warm and high-spirited. But others are lost." She turned and stared into his eyes. "They need to have faith. They are hungry for compassion."

"And you?"

She looked back at the sunset. "What do you mean?"

Juan raised his eyebrow. "Emotional satisfaction?"

"If you mean sensual gratification, compassion for God is all I need."

A smile came over his face as he gazed at the sunset.

"Why? Don't you have compassion for the Lord? Dr. Sanchez?"

He turned toward her. "And you can call me Juan." He thought for a moment. "There is more to life than just the Lord. Don't misunderstand. I was the product of a Catholic family in Spain. But we are here to do other things than focus on the Lord." He smirks at her. "I believe God is an entity with no personal involvement in our everyday lives."

"So, God is impersonal?"

"I suppose you can say that."

"I see."

"Don't take it personally."

"Oh no. Not at all. That is your conviction."

"Tell me, Diana. Why would a young woman abstain from the social pleasures of life to serve God?"

"And why did you decide to serve as a volunteer, leaving behind a promising career as a doctor?"

"To help those less fortunate. It's my Hippocratic oath."

"Well, you could have done so back home. Why here?"

"I believed I could best serve my oath by volunteering as a doctor for the Red Cross."

"I, too, have an oath to fulfill. An oath a young woman decides to take to be a Sister for the Lord. My oath, like yours, brought me here. The difference is, your oath is humanitarian, while mine is spiritual."

They gazed into each other's eyes as if lost in their thoughts. Juan decided to speak.

"Diana. I think... Oh, never mind."

"No. Tell me."

"It is something I should not be thinking about. After all, you are a Sister."

"Are you sure?"

Juan felt uneasy about his sudden desire for her. "Yes. I should go." Juan began to leave but stopped to address her. "I have an engagement with a colleague of mine, but I will see you tomorrow."

"I'll be here attending to my patients."

"Your patients? You speak as if you are their doctor. Or should I say their keeper?"

"God is our only true keeper."

Juan smiled and walked away. Diana followed him with her eyes.

The following day, the nuns visited a grocery market in the center of Pretoria. They were dressed in their black habits shopping at the local store. Although small, the store was sufficiently stocked with staple foodstuffs, produce, dairy products, household supplies, and non-prescription medication. Dorothy and Gertrude stood by the canned goods shelf.

Dorothy examined a can of kangaroo meat as she held it in her hand. "I wonder if I should try this kangaroo meat for our Easter dinner, Sister Gertrude?"

"I have never indulged in it before, Sister Dorothy. You certainly will not find it back home in Ireland."

Dorothy placed the can back on the shelf. "I think I will pass on this one." She continued working the shelf, examining the various cans with Gertrude. "So, did anything interesting happen at the hospital the other day?"

"There was this one daring little African lad who came down with chicken pox. He was such a cute little lad. But he found my attire rather interesting."

"That's because he probably never witnessed a nun before."

Gertrude added. "Many of the Africans are not familiar with our faith."

Dorothy injected, "I think a little discipleship is in order. I noticed the chapel at the hospital is not in use. It is in bad need of repairs. But I was told the hospital is short of funds. We could remedy that problem."

"Yes. We can use it as a place of spiritual discipleship."

"Precisely, Sister Gertrude."

"But Sister Dorothy. I am not very good with the hammer."

Suddenly, Adeline approached, holding a live desert tortoise. The desert tortoise appeared quite docile in her hands.

Dorothy raised her eyebrows. "And what in the name are you doing with this turtle, Sister Adeline?"

"It's a desert tortoise."

"And what are we going to do with it?"

"Eat it."

"Eat it?"

"It's considered a delicacy."

Gertrude took a closer look at the reptile. "It appears harmless. Almost docile looking."

"And who is going to cook this desert tortoise?"

I will, Sister Dorothy. Well... actually. It will be Sister Diana doing the cooking."

"Sister Diana! I should have known."

Diana approached them. "They are considered a delicacy here."

She took the tortoise from Adeline. Dorothy looked sternly at Diana and Adeline before gazing at the desert tortoise. The tortoise looked back at Dorothy as if studying her.

"Oh. Very well. Come on. Let's go." Dorothy walked away with Gertrude, Diana, and Adeline following, carrying the tortoise.

The nuns were gathered by the counter as the Grocer, in his mid-50s with a Dutch accent, bagged their food. Adeline carried the desert tortoise in a small wooden cage.

"It's nice to see a group of nuns around here."

Dorothy's serious face managed a smile. "Why, thank you."

Diana, Gertrude, and Elizabeth each retrieved a bag from the grocer.

"So, all of you are volunteers at the hospital?"

Gertrude is quick with the answer. "That's right."

"Nuns working at the hospital."

Helen was agitated. "We just said that."

"So, if I needed a check-up, I come see one of you. Ya?"

Elizabeth giggled. "Actually. Diana is the only nurse here."

"That would be me."

"Ah... Is that a fact? So, the prettiest sister here will be doing the checking."

The nuns giggled.

Helen, on the other hand, displayed a look of disgust on her face. "I believe the doctor will be doing the examination."

"Oh. Too bad."

Dorothy had enough. "We must be on our way. Come."

Dorothy began to leave. The other nuns follow.

"Bye. Hope to see you all very soon."

Elizabeth answered with a cackle. "Bye."

Leaving the store, the nuns decided to walk down the pavement and observe the downtown streets bustling with activity. People walked, rode on horseback, and drove their horse-drawn carriages.

Diana suddenly spotted Juan having a lively conversation with a man a short distance away. Helen noticed.

"Tell me, Sister Diana, how is it working with your doctor friend?"

"Doctor Sanchez?"

"I believe that's the one."

Adeline and Elizabeth giggled as the nuns continued their walk.

"Oh. I would not call him a friend."

"Then what would you call him?"

"A physician."

Helen's eyebrows pulled up, "Ha! I've seen the sultry look you gave him."

"What do you mean?"

"Do not fool me. Just remember, Sister, you have yet to take your vows. Do you not want the temptation to jeopardize your sisterhood?"

Dorothy raised her chin. "Now, Sister Helen!"

Suddenly, they reached a street corner. However, they could not cross the street because a horse-driven milk wagon blocked their path. The nuns patiently waited until the wagon cleared the corner.

Elizabeth revealed a flirtatious smile. "He is so cute."

Gertrude interjected. "I think it is time to change the subject."

There was silence as their eyes were fixed on the wagon. Unexpectedly, Diana turned. She saw Juan continue to talk to the gentleman as they crossed the street. Their conversation was mixed with laughter. However, Juan did not notice Diana was staring at him. Diana's face became radiant as she continued to stare at him. The wagon finally left, clearing the way for the nuns to continue their walk. The nuns make their way with Dorothy, Gertrude, and Elizabeth chit-chatting as the other

CHAPTER 6 – A NEW BEGINNING

nuns listen. However, Diana's mind was elsewhere, as her face was still glowing.

Every day for the next two weeks, Diana and Juan worked closely together at the hospital from early morning to late at night. This close relationship caused Diana to become more attached to him. For instance, Juan would administer vaccine shots to a line of walking patients, with Diana assisting. However, Diana's eyes focused mainly on Juan, as she glanced at his face at every opportunity.

The patients said hello to Diana as they received their shots. Diana relied only with a quick smile as she focused on Juan, who was too busy to notice Diana's wanting stares.

A short time later, Diana and Juan gathered some medical supplies from a wagon in front of the hospital. However, Diana's actions with the doctor appeared flirtatious. Pedestrians walking past them noticed her actions. Some were surprised, while others smiled.

Later in the afternoon, Diana and Juan visited some sick children in the pediatric ward. Juan picked up a little boy and held him in his arms. He began conversing with the boy. Meanwhile, Diana admired Juan and noticed how wonderful he was with children.

Late in the evening, Diana and Juan were in an operating room, Juan attending to a wounded commando. Diana assisted him, holding a sponge in her hand. Juan made an insertion in the soldier's torso. Diana wiped perspiration from Juan's forehead. She kept her eyes fixed on Juan as he continued to operate.

It is now nightfall, and Diana and Juan went to a courtyard in the hospital with children around them. Suddenly, the children notice some carnations sprouting from the ground. Juan nonchalantly picked several of them and handed them to Diana in a thoughtful manner. The children created a spectacle as they gleeed. A fellow doctor then entered and went to Juan. Juan had to excuse himself and left with the doctor, leaving Diana standing with the children. Holding the carnations, Diana looked at the flowers and towards Juan's departing like a love-smitten schoolgirl. Diana's passion for Juan was indeed growing. She knew this, but could not prevent it as she continued working with him.

CHAPTER 7 – TURNING POINT

The following day, Diana was attending to her nursing duties in the isolation area at Volks Hospital. She was with a Boer patient in his 20s named Dirck Verkuilen. He lay in bed and was dying because of his wounds, which did not heal correctly from a battle he had been in. Because of this, his injuries developed into necrotic wounds. Although young, his face looked worn. He talked to Diana in his Dutch accent. Diana sat next to him and tried to give him comfort. Dressed in her usual nurse attire with her veil, she listened to him attentively as she held his hand.

"Do you need anything? Maybe a glass of water?"

Dirck began to cough. Diana touched his forehead. She then reached for the stethoscope around her neck and checked his heart rate. Dirck began to cough again.

"How am I?"

"Everything is fine, Dirck."

"Don't lie. You know I will die soon."

Diana replied by giving him a glass of water. He drank.

"I thought my wounds were patched, and didn't think I would have to come back here anymore." Dirck coughed again.

"In what battle did you receive your wounds?"

"Elandslaagte."

"Elandslaagte?"

"Yes. It is near Ladysmith. The battle went all wrong for us. Though the British did leave after they won." Dirck coughed again.

"You don't have to say anymore."

"No. It's all right, Diana." He cleared his throat." Our objective was simple. General Kock was supposed to blow up the railway lines in Natal. Instead, we occupied the railway station at Elandslaagte, cutting off communication for the main British forces. ..."

Dirck described the battle to Diana. It was in full swing, with about one thousand Boer militia positioned behind a ridge two miles southeast of the railroad station. The ridge formed into a horseshoe shape, approximately three miles in length. It rose about 100 feet above the plain. The northern end of the ridge dropped sharply and rose again at a much lower point. It ran south as it dipped into a grassy hollow. Along the southern crest of the ridge was a barbed-wire fence.

The Boer tried to keep some 3,000 British infantry and cavalry from overtaking the ridge.

A huge black, purplish thundercloud hung over the battlefield. Due to the ominous cloud, rifle and cannon fire were easily visible against the background. Behind the ridge was the Boer camp. Some Boer men run ammunition to the Boer sharpshooters from the camp.

The Boers fire their 75mm creusots at the British artillery positions. Boer cannons, which number only three, were a short distance behind the ridge. A few on their shells manage to make direct hits. One in particular hit a supply wagon, causing debris to fly in the air.

Meanwhile, some 3,000 yards from the railroad station, the British 15-pound guns bear down on the Boer. They had 18 in all. A direct hit from a British artillery shell blew away several Boer sharpshooters. About 1,000 yards from the ridge, Boer rifle power pinned the British troops down.

Termite Hills at Elandslaagte, one of the British groups, was the Devonshire infantry regiment on the right side of the ridge. They took cover behind large heaps on Termite Hills. Two newspaper correspondents wearing civilian clothes were with the regiment, Bennett and Melton, both in their late 20s. Milton sported a Blanco's solar topee. They cover the battle for the London Times. However, they were coming under heavy fire from Boer positions on the ridge.

Bennett was confused; the Boer commandoes were shooting at them. "Why are they shooting at us so much?"

Milton replied. "Hell, if I know."

Bennett turned at Milton, and realized the problem. "It's that damn topee. It makes a perfect target. Take it off!"

"What?"

"Take it off?" Bennett repeated.

Several bullets fly right by the correspondents again.

"I don't want to be yesterday's news!"

Without saying another word, Melton took his topee from his head. The bullet fire stopped.

"Now that's more like it." Bennett commended with a sense of relief.

Behind Elandslaagte Natal Ridge, Dirck carried on his back a young Boer soldier named Kirk, who was mortally wounded in the leg.

"Don't worry, Kirk. You will be safe and sound."

Unexpectedly, a British shell landed a short distance away, knocking Dirck and Kirk to the ground. Kirk immediately cried out in pain. Undaunted, Dirck went over and picked up Kirk again. On his back, Dirck hurriedly went to a nearby makeshift wagon serving as an ambulance. Kirk reached to touch his wounded leg. He again lets out a cry.

"Don't touch it! Don't touch it!"

Kirk continued to cry out. "It's going to be cut off! I know it."

"Shut up, you fool."

A Boer on horseback came and pulled a wagon. Dirck placed Kirk in the wagon, and the wagon left. Dirck also left, looking for safe cover.

Meanwhile, the British batteries start to pour down their shelling on the south side of the ridge. The Boer troops begin to retreat from the area in haste. Some were blown away by heavy artillery fire.

A handful of British officers and soldiers reach the barbed wire fence. One of the officers was Captain Haldane, while the other was Major Denne. With wire cutters in hand, they begin to cut the wire. Private Fraser, a big husky fellow, began to pull the wires apart with his bare hands. He caused significant gaps. Large enough for a small group of men to go through. Suddenly, several Boers fire their Mauser rifles down on them. Several British foot soldiers fired back. However, one British soldier was hit in the chest as he fell to the ground close to Private Fraser. Colonel Cunningham rode up on his horse and saw gaps in the fence. He shouted and waved to the Natal Mounted Rifles B squadron of about 150 men, a short distance away.

"On men! It's time to attack."

Suddenly, Cunningham was shot in the arm by a Boer commando and fell off his horse. The men storm the fence. They cross into the ridge in open territory. Meanwhile, a hundred yards away, some 50 Boer militia begin a counterattack, firing their rifles. Several British soldiers fell, while others decided to retreat through the open fence. The Boers continue their fire.

Colonel Hamilton rode up. "Fix bayonets, Charge!"

The Drum Major of the 2nd Gordon Highlanders sounded a bugle to charge. The

British infantry regrouped and charged again; this time being led by the Imperial Light Cavalry. Charging with their pistols in their hands, they fire at the Boer. Behind the cavalry, the dismounted B squadron approached. Overwhelmed by the charging cavalry, the small band of Boer militia retreated. Many were killed instantly by the charging cavalry. A few Boers show white flags.

General Kock led a surprise counterattack down the hillside, dressed in his top hat and Sunday best with forty commandos. He began to drive back the infantry. Hamilton ordered the British Bugler and Pipers to sound the charge again. The infantry recharged. Kock was seriously wounded as he and his men were hit with a wall of bullets.

British 5th Lancers, numbering several hundred, begin charging up the ridge's northern side. However, Boer sharpshooters repel the frontal assault with their rifle fire. A small number of Lancers were hit in the head and facial area. Their lifeless bodies, with their stretched-out lances, plummet to the ground. The other Lancers decided to retreat and charge again. The ominous cloud began to produce rain on the battlefield.

The Devonshire regiment charged up to the north side of the ridge. Their rifle fire managed to hit some of the Boer marksmen. The Boer militia shouted in pain.

The mounted cavalry of the 5th Dragoon Guards raced across the south side through what

CHAPTER 7 – TURNING POINT

was once a wire fence. With their swords waving in the air, they begin to chase down hundreds of Boer soldiers who retreated to the north end of the ridge.

The Lancers attempted another charge, but this time they were successful. Their horses gallop over the crest line. The Boers shot some Lancers, who remained on the crest line. A Boer manages to knock a Lancer off his horse with the butt of his rifle. However, the majority of Lancers made their way with their lances. Most of the Boers began to run, some throwing their rifles to the ground. However, the Lancers ram their lances through their retreating bodies. A horse with two Boers galloped away. A Lancer approached them and rammed his lance through the two Boers with one thrust.

Meanwhile, Dirck decided to run into an underbrush. However, a British infantry soldier hit Dirck in the back with a solid shot, causing him to fall to the ground. Dirck managed to crawl to the underbrush on his stomach.

The 5th Dragoon Guards hack away at the retreating Boer militia. A guard managed to decapitate a fleeing Boer. A group of Lancers rounded up about 50 Boer soldiers as their hands were raised in the air in surrender. One of the prisoners was a woman who accompanied her Boer husband. The group of Lancers surrounded their prisoners, who fell to their knees with their hands still raised. Suddenly, a Lancer officer shouts to the Lancers and, without warning, thrusts their lances through their bodies. The Lancers seem to glee at their merciless act.

Colonel Hamilton finally arrived at the crest of the ridge with the rest of the infantry. He quickly noticed dead bodies everywhere. He saw that the Boer camp had raised the white flag to surrender. He ordered a bugler to sound the call for a cease-fire. The bugler played the sound, and the British cavalry suddenly stopped their vicious attacks.

Suddenly, a small group of armed Boers emerged from behind the camp and began shooting at the British. However, the infantry quickly responded with a wall of firing bullets. Most fell to their death. A few managed to throw down their weapons and began to retreat wildly.

Several Lancers began to chase them, but Colonel Hamilton immediately ordered the bugler to sound the order to cease. The Lancers stop dead in their tracks as the bugler sounds the call—a look of disappointment registered on their bloodthirsty faces.

The two news correspondents finally make their way up to the crest of the battlefield as the rain suddenly stops. They were shocked to find the carnage spread about. They saw the dead prisoners as the Lancers continued to glee.

Melton looked around. "Were there not prisoners?"

Bennett was also puzzled at the site. "They must be. They were not armed. Many fled, leaving their weapons. So, there should be."

Milton then realized the brutality of the slaughter. "My word. I cannot believe we came to see such brutal acts."

Bennett echoed his sentiment. "I do not think this is something for print in the London Times."

Milton and Bennett continued to stare at the dead. They could hear the groans of the badly wounded calling out for help. Among the dead was an elderly Boer on the ground cradling his 13-year-old son, also killed in the battle.

On his horse, a glum look was written all over Hamilton's face as he stared in complete horror at the wounded and dead on the ground. Some dead British soldiers and Boer commandos were intermingled.

A wounded Dirck still lay behind the brush. Tears fell from his dirt-ridden face as he witnessed the horror of battle and the bloody massacre.

The British did manage to capture some retreating Boer soldiers as they raised their hands without killing them. One of them was Cornelis Vincent 'Cor' van Gogh, the brother of Vincent van Gogh. However, he died later after he was hospitalized. But the brother of another famous Dutch artist, Piet Mondrian, taken prisoner after the battle, managed to live.

Back at Volks hospital, Dirck laid in bed as he had finished his story. Tears were running down Diana's face. Dirck smiled at Diana. And without warning, he closed his eyes and died. Diana reached to feel for a pulse but could not find one. She retrieved a rosary from her pocket and gently placed it on top of the chest of Dirck's dead body. She looked up, searching for something to say in prayer. But she could not come up with the words, as she was too gripped with sorrow. She leaned over and kissed him on the forehead. She stood and walked away dispirited.

Down a dark hallway at the hospital, with a few kerosene lamps providing light, Diana was in tears. Juan entered from the other end of the hallway. She suddenly saw him walking towards her. She decided to run to him. They embraced. Juan was puzzled by Diana's emotions, yet he found comfort in hugging her. She looked up at him.

"What's wrong, Diana?"

"I heard such a horrible story."

"Oh?"

"A patient that I came to know told me about a battle he was in. The slaughter. The destruction. Dead lying everywhere. Why do we have to continue killing each other?"

"Diana. Everything will be all right. Did you not say that one must have faith?"

Diana left his embrace, rubbing her eyes. Juan pulled a handkerchief out of his coat pocket and gave it to her. She wiped away her tears.

"I know what I said. I just never expected it would be like this. I haven't had the slightest clue of what war would be like. I read about it in history books. But this ...how long will it continue?"

"You are strong. I see how you communicate with the patients. They look up to you. You are their ray of sunshine. Their last hope for redemption before they meet death in this war."

Without saying a word, Diana looked at him. Her sadness turned to a longing for him. Without warning, they began to kiss. Their kiss was timid yet tender. Their lips met again as they embraced each other. But this time, it was much more passionate. Suddenly, Juan pulled away from Diana.

"I can't."

He turned, and he began to walk away. However, after a few steps, he turned back toward Diana as she held his handkerchief.

"You know I am falling in love with you. And here I am, trying to be a nun. You think I do not know the consequences of my acts." She gathered herself. "When I first met you. I found you to be quite charming. Maybe your looks. Maybe your smile. But as time went on. I found a maturity and strength in you that I could hold on to. Is that so wrong? Is it wrong to love? To love someone?"

Juan did not reply, as he was at a loss for words.

"Some will say, one can serve God with all their heart and still love another."

Juan smiled. "And what does your heart say?"

"That I can."

Juan approached her. "You once told me you were above all this."

"Yes. I said a great many things."

Juan touched her face and softly kissed her lips. He wanted to kiss her again, but he decided not to. He turned and walked away. Diana looked at him as tears began to spill down her cheeks again.

The following afternoon, the nuns met at the hospital's run-down chapel. The chapel was small, with about twenty pews, ten on each side of the aisle. Sunlight spilled in through several small windows, overlooking the courtyard. Since the chapel was unfinished, the nuns were repairing it the best they could, except for Helen, who was absent. Gertrude and Adeline repainted part of a wall, with Adeline perched on a ladder. Diana held a piece of wood steady on a saw horse as Elizabeth diligently cut away with a saw. Dorothy nailed a piece of trim wood around a window.

Dorothy stopped and looked at Adeline's progress. "Sister Adeline. You miss a spot."

"Where?"

"Over there to your left. Just above your head."

Adeline looked in that direction and noticed the unpainted spot. She quickly brushed some fresh white paint over it, and Dorothy continued to nail.

Gertrude slapped some paint on the wall. "It's

too bad Sister Helen could not make it, Sister Dorothy."

"She says she might be coming down with the flu."

Adeline stopped her painting. "That's odd. Sister Diana and I saw her playing badminton this morning."

The piece of wood Elizabeth has been sawing fell to the floor. "Here's another piece, Sister Dorothy."

"Just lay it over here."

Elizabeth retrieved the wood. She walked over and laid it by Dorothy as she continued to nail away.

Adeline continued painting. "I believe this shall be a lovely place when we finish. And it will be ready for Easter."

"I believe so, too," Dorothy said with a smile,

Elizabeth placed the saw on an empty pew and sat next to it. Diana lifted the sawhorse and carried it to a nearby wall. She then retrieved a jar of varnish and a couple of rags and walked over to Elizabeth.

"Here." She handed Elizabeth a rag.

"When do we take a break?"

"When we finish, Sister Elizabeth."

"I heard resting the body after a few hours of hard work is good for the soul."

Gertrude grinned. "That is for non-believers,

Sister Elizabeth."

Elizabeth lets out a giggle. "Oh. You are right." She stood and went back to work.

Dorothy reassured Elizabeth. "Do not worry, Sister. Our first break will be coming soon enough."

Diana raised the jar as if to pour. Receiving the hint, Elizabeth laid out her rag, and Diana began to pour some vanish on the cloth. Elizabeth let out another giggle.

"Thanks."

Diana walked over to the other side of the aisle, poured varnish on her rag, and began to rub the pew.

Adeline turned to Elizabeth. "The saw?"

Elizabeth let out another giggle. "Oh, silly me." Elizabeth went over and placed the saw on the floor. She then began to varnish a pew.

Gertrude beamed, "Before long. This place will be bustling with activity."

Adeline added. "To help the wounded."

Gertrude said, "It was nice of the carpenter to cover up that awful hole this morning. I mean it was large enough for all of us to fall in."

Dorothy paused her nailing. "Yes. Remind me to lift him in prayer. He received word the other day that his son was wounded."

A somber look came over Gertrude. "Dear. I hope it is not fatal."

CHAPTER 7 – TURNING POINT

Adeline changed the subject. "It's unfortunate this could not be accomplished any sooner."

Elizabeth was all smiles. "Just think of the hope and peace this chapel will bring for all those who have loved ones fighting and those who have died."

Suddenly, Diana stopped rubbing the pew and appeared lost in thought, thinking of Dirck and the ordeal of the battle.

Dorothy turned to her. "Diana. You have not said much today. Is everything all right?"

Gertrude interjected. "You know Sister Diana. She always has things on her mind."

The nuns giggled at her remarks and continued to work. Diana wiped the rag against the pew, still lost in thought.

Several days later, Diana was at the local cemetery in Pretoria. The cemetery appeared barren of visitors, as hundreds of stone markers and wooden crosses marked the graves of the dead. The cemetery was deserted, save for Diana. She stood alone before a small headstone, wearing her black habit and holding a dozen red roses.

The headstone read "DIRCK VERKUILEN". Diana laid the roses in front of Dirck's grave. She stared at Dirck's headstone. She then looked at all the dead markers around her. She then sang as if singing to the dead.

"So many have died in the field
They fight for their cause

They fight for their honor
They fight for a burning passion
They fight for a calling deep inside
And yet, many died in the field

Love is what we should strive for
A love to bring hope and sunshine
Love to bring everlasting peace
A rainbow leading us without sorrow
To see things in a much different way
To live to love. To love to live

So many have died in the field
They fight for their cause
They fight for their honor
They fight for a burning passion
They fight for a calling deep inside
And yet, many died in the field

Love is what we should strive for
To be free of all evil things
To see a better life of happiness
Not to have many dying in the field
 Where peace will prevail for us all
 To live to love. To love to live."

She then looked around one more time at the sea of dead markers and walked away in despair.

The chapel was in fine shape for an early April Easter, as some hundred patients and medical staff sat in the pews. They sang a song from their

CHAPTER 7 – TURNING POINT

hymnals as Dorothy played the piano. A banner was pinned on the wall above the piano, "Happy Easter." Diana and Gertrude led the singing as they stood before the pews. Helen and Elizabeth were busy doing administrative duties and could not attend the chapel. Adeline sat next to a patient in the front pew. She held a hymnal for her as they both sang.

Suddenly, Juan walked into the chapel and immediately stood against a wall. With a smile, he was happy to see the nuns' progress with the patients and the chapel. Diana noticed Juan as she turned in his direction. She was surprised but glad. Diana and Juan managed to smile at each other. Diana continued to sing with the patients but glanced at Juan.

Several days later, it was a fine morning. Juan was up early and felt a new life was waiting for him, as he looked at the landscape from his quarters. Despite the war tearing the country apart, beauty can still be found in South Africa. Hope it seems, was not lost despite the bloody conflict. Likewise, Juan saw hope in front of him in the name D-I-A-N-A. He longed for her. Wanting to touch her, desiring to make love to her. Each passing day working with her at the hospital just made the desire for her stronger. Yet he knew how wrong it was to long for her as he did. He was brought up as a Catholic. And he knew Diana was forbidden fruit.

But there she was, a tempting fruit waiting to be bitten into. And there he was, wanting her and knowing how wrong it was to want her the way he did. Although in his mid-30s, Juan had his share of women. Spanish señoritas, with their exotic looks and sensual smiles. Their beauty was undeniable. But Juan never came around and married one of them. And there were many. No. Juan was too busy with his medical practice to settle down. His good looks and romantic charm made them easy conquests for the dashing doctor.

He searched his soul, trying to find a way out of his predicament. This twisted desire he had for Diana. Falling for her. He either avoided love or did not find the right woman for this love. Besides, marriage did not interest him. He was having fun with the many women he socialized with. He was still young, and a future wife could wait. He only volunteered to aid the Red Cross because he wanted to travel, and working at the Volks hospital would give him the surgical experience he could take back to Spain. Advanced his career as a surgeon. However, Diana was different. She had an exceptional beauty and a spirit he had not seen before. Maybe because she was from a different culture? Or perhaps it was because she had a way of bringing a smile to the patients around her in the most difficult times. Juan would work on the operating table to save as many people as possible, and Diana would work tirelessly beside him, never complaining.

Juan wanted to seduce her. But he knew it would be wrong. And if he tried, what would she do? How would she react? After all, she was studying to be a nun. And by chance, if he was successful. How long would the affair last? He would lose his ability to practice at the hospital, and the sisterhood would chastise Diana. Probably never allowing her to be a nun. But what did it matter if two people genuinely love each other? Love conquers all. Right? So, Juan needed to find out where she stood. But he wanted her to make the first move. Juan felt she would remove her veil and disrobe her habit for him if he created the right moment. To see if she was really the woman of his dreams. His future wife.

Later in the morning, at Volks Hospital, Ruth was checking in patients at the ward when Juan approached her.

"Since Van is sick today, I will go for the hospital supplies."

"But what about your patients?"

"Dr. Visser can cover for me."

She reflected for a moment. "All right."

Juan was about to leave, but turned toward her. "I forgot to mention, Diana will be with me."

"Diana?"

"I will need some assistance, and she volunteered."

Ruth looked rather suspiciously at Juan. "Hmmm. I see." She sternly looks into his eyes. "Well, you best get going."

Ruth walked away. Juan smiled.

Diana and Juan sat together as they rode a small covered wagon down a neighborhood street in Pretoria. Juan pulled the two horses. They passed small shops and houses as a few pedestrians walked by, attending to their business. Diana was dressed in her habit today, with Juan in street clothes.

Juan kept his eyes on the road. "Remember. We are to have a relaxing day. Like talking. Nothing more."

"My sentiments exactly." Diana looked up. "My. It's such a beautiful day. Not a cloud in the sky."

Juan turned and admiringly looked at Diana. "Yes, it sure is."

They both managed to smile at each other as they continued on their journey.

Diana and Juan were in a secluded place on a grassy hillside, sitting on a tablecloth underneath a tree. Their lunch, which consisted of a basket of fruits, baked bread, and a bottle of wine, was spread before them. Diana and Juan sipped their wine and nibbled on their food.

Diana queried. "So, all this fighting is about gold?"

"Well, in a roundabout way. Yes."

"How much gold?"

"No one knows for sure. The discovered mines are so vast."

"They could not settle their differences peacefully?"

"And you would have?"

"I would say. Now, you British share half the gold with the Boer government. And you, Boer, share half the gold with the British."

"It would be that simple, Diana?"

"Why yes, Juan. You said it was about gold?"

"Well. It's a little more complicated than that. Political and cultural issues are at play."

"The same God creates us all. We should not have any problems dealing with trivial differences? I tend to think men tend to make things complicated."

"So, you have an issue concerning men?"

"I admire men in authority. After all, our Pope has always been a man. But most men would rather settle their differences with a sword rather than a handshake."

"Maybe some things can only be settled with a sword."

Diana replied as she smirked. She took a sip. "I heard that Boer means farmer in Dutch."

"Yes. The Dutch were the first Europeans to settle this land. And now they are fighting to keep their republics free of British encroachments."

"So, you are sympathetic to the Boer?"

"To a degree. But, like you, I wish for the fighting to end."

After taking another sip, she warmly smiled at him. "I normally do not partake in the fermented grape. Except for mass, of course."

Juan also replied with a warm smile. "A little wine is good for the soul."

Diana and Juan giggled. She laid a hand next to Juan. Juan, in turn, decided to place his hand over hers gently. They stare at each other in almost frozen silence.

"I assume you will return to Ireland when all this is over?"

"I have planned it so." She turned away for a moment and looked back at him." I remember first laying eyes on you at the train at Vereeniging."

"I was not planning to be involved with anyone."

Diana studied his eyes. "You mean fall in love?"

"You know what I am trying to say." Juan began to feel uneasy. "It just doesn't feel right. To have desires for a sister of the Catholic faith."

Juan took his hand away. Diana's good cheer vanished.

Diana and Juan sat back on the covered wagon

after finishing their picnic. Juan turned to Diana. Without saying another word, Juan reached for Diana. They began to kiss passionately.

"I wish I could do more than just kiss you. I want to carry you in my arms and love you. To satisfy the feelings in me. To satisfy the feelings we have for each other."

"Yes, I do too. But I am a sister of a faith you still hold dear." She looked more closely into his eyes. "Maybe it is best to end it here. Here and now."

Juan seemed to be lost in her eyes. "Are you sure?"

"No."

They again kiss passionately.

Juan then kissed her neck, and then part of her face. "I could not stop seeing you."

Diana did not pull back. "Nor I you."

They continued kissing.

The following evening, Diana and another nurse, Paula, in her 30s, cleaned surgical instruments with a sanitation washbasin and wore disposable gloves after treating the wounded at the hospital. Diana noticed the wall clock. She turned to Paula.

"Paula, can you finish for me? I have an appointment I must attend to."

"Sure, Diana. No problem."

"Many thanks."

Diana pulled off her gloves and tossed them in a trash can. She quickly left. She went to a dressing area in the hospital to change into her black habit.

Later that night, Diana, wearing her habit, stood alone in an abandoned warehouse in Pretoria. Other than the moonlight, there was no other source of light. She looked impatient and somewhat tense. Suddenly, Juan entered. They immediately saw each other, and Diana went to Juan. They embrace each other, and they kiss. They look at each other passionately and kiss again. They stopped, and Juan quickly lit several kerosene lamps attached to a nearby wall.

He approached her again. "I miss you. Even though our picnic was only yesterday."

"I was afraid I might be seen."

Juan looked into her eyes. "I'm glad you came. I need you so much. Like dry grass needs rain. Or like the clouds need the sky. I know you are risking everything to be with me."

"And you with me."

They decide to kiss.

"I knew no one would be here."

Diana turned and looked at the empty vastness.

Juan continued, "Before the war, this place would be stocked with wool, waiting to be exported to foreign markets. But now that the British Navy has blockaded South Africa, this thriving business is no more." Juan then reached into his coat pocket. "I have something to give you."

CHAPTER 7 – TURNING POINT

"Oh?"

A closer look revealed a necklace with a medallion of a baby's shoe. The shoe was made of copper, with a shining diamond on its front.

"I want you to have this." He handed it to her.

She looked at it in wonder. "It's a shoe, and with a diamond! It is so exquisite!"

"I was born into a very poor family. My deceased mother used to stand by a shoe store every morning with me in her arms, asking for money. Being an infant, she thought it would bring sympathy. She noticed how I would fix my eyes on a pair of beautiful baby shoes she could not afford."

Diana affectionately touched the neckline, as Juan continued. "It was not until several years later that I wore my first pair of shoes. After my mother remarried, she gave me this necklace and asked for forgiveness for not buying me those shoes my little eyes wanted when I was in her arms. And now I want you to have this."

With her eyes fixed on the diamond, Diana placed the necklace around her neck. She looked down at the diamond. "The diamond is so beautiful."

"Diamonds are very affordable in South Africa, so I decided to place one on the shoe."

"It looks expensive."

"The jeweler said it is several carats."

Diana embraces Juan. "I feel so happy inside. I just want to dance."

"Dance?"

"Yes. Dance." Diana pulled away from Juan. "Happiness does this to me sometimes."

"What kind of dancing?"

"Irish. What else?"

"Show me."

"Show you! Now?"

"You said you felt like dancing."

Diana looked around the warehouse.

"How much room do you need?"

"Oh. It's plenty enough." She gathered herself. "All right then." Diana moved away from Juan and stood at a short distance. She raised her shirt and began to kick up her heels. She moved with grace and energy, performing her dancing. Her body was in the rhythm of her Irish step dancing. Juan began to clap. This excited Diana, and she decided to pick up her tempo, covering the ground. She changed the style of her steps but continued with the same intensity. As Diana continued, she raised her shirt even higher, exposing her thighs. This, of course, delighted Juan. Continuing her dance, she danced up to him.

"Come on."

"Me?"

"I will make you Irish yet, my Spanish conquistador."

Diana slowed down her steps to make it easier for Juan to follow. Without breaking stride, she took Juan's hands. They continued, but it was difficult for him.

She sang to him as she tried to guide him.

"If you want to dance
Just flow with me some
Step-by-step and motion-to-motion
Step-by-step and motion-to-motion."

But Juan almost lost his composure. Diana kept him in stride. She sang.

"If you want to dance
Just flow with me some
It is not hard to do if you let go
For its step-by-step and motion-to-motion."

They continued slowly as Diana guided him. Juan watched his feet as he began to move with her.

Diana continued to sing.

"And as you dance, you feel free
Free to move around
Free to be with me
For its step-by-step and motion-to-motion."

They dance hand in hand as they cover the ground. Juan did his best to dance with Diana, following her steps. His dancing was not on par with Diana's, but it was not bad for a beginner. Diana decided to stop and applaud Juan for his efforts.

"I will get used to this Irish dancing. But have you ever heard of the tango?"

"I know of this dance. But I have not performed it."

"Let me show you."

Juan brought Diana close to his chest as he held her hands in a close embrace.

"Just follow my steps."

Diana did not say a word, smiling at him. He took small steps and began rhythmic footwork. He began to move around the floor, with Diana keeping up with him. He then spun her, and she complied with ease. They continued dancing. He then captured Diana's foot with his and swept her foot along the floor. Juan then continued with several tango moves, which Diana was able to adapt to. Juan then grabbed her and lifted her off the ground. He placed her down on the ground, and they stared into each other's eyes. They proceeded to kiss with passion.

The following day, staff and visitors ate at the hospital mess hall. The nuns walked to an empty, long table with their food tray and sat. Diana sat next to Elizabeth and Gertrude.

Elizabeth turned to Diana. "Sister Diana. Can you pass me the salt?"

"Why certainly." She reached over and handed Elizabeth the salt container.

"Why, thank you."

Dorothy said. "I heard a marvelous story this morning."

Adeline's face lit up. "Oh, please tell us, Sister!"

Elizabeth is all smiles. "Yes, please do."

"Well, according to this worker named Peepado."

Helen's eyes narrowed. "Peepado?"

"Yes. He's from an African village just outside Johannesburg. Well, it's closer to Pretoria. By the way, is not Peepado a charming name?"

Helen sounded indifferent. "If you say so."

"Well. This hospital worker's name is Peepado..."

As Dorothy continued with her conversation. Diana saw Juan sitting with several doctors, eating a short distance away. He turned and noticed her as well. Their eyes locked. Sensual smiles came over them. Like Diana, Juan was not interested in the conversation at his table.

A week later, Diana and Juan had the day to themselves. The other nuns assumed Diana was on a hospital assignment off-site. Diana was off-site, but it was not a hospital assignment. She was riding horseback with Juan in some rural area near Pretoria. They rode the horses in a slow gait. She was wearing her black habit and looked comfortable on the horse.

"So, what did you tell your Sisters today?"

"I told them I was working this Sunday on a hospital assignment. At this moment, they are attending Mass and then will conduct a rosary afterward." She frowned. "I know it was a naughty thing for me to do."

"Naughty, no. You wanted to go where your heart led you. What is naughty about that?"

"But the Sisters would not see it this way."

"Does it matter what they see?"

"They are blinded by their habits. The sisterhood, as you call it." Diana reflected for a moment. "True sensual love with another human soul will always pass them by." She stopped her horse. This caused Juan to stop his.

"Have you ever been in love before, Juan?"

"I have had my share."

"I see." Diana continued with her horse. Likewise, Juan did the same.

"But I do not know if I can measure up to the other women in your past life. After all, a man like you has probably experienced many women."

Juan cleared his throat. "I was with a few. But what does that matter?"

Diana again stopped her horse, and Juan stopped his. Diana did not utter a word; she looked at him with melancholy.

"Is it your virginity? Afraid you will not measure up to the adventurous women of my past?"

CHAPTER 7 – TURNING POINT

"I just want to make sure you are sure."

"I have yet to admire your total beauty. Yet I already know what I already know."

"I feel so inadequate. Not a complete woman."

Juan reached for her hand and gently kissed it.

"Innocent beauty. You are more than all the women I've known before. And all that I will ever know."

He reached for her. They kiss while on their horses.

Later in the afternoon, Diana and Juan walked hand in hand as they talked in a field of many sunflowers on a nice day, with their horses following close behind. They laughed and delightfully joked with each other.

Diana then sat on a large rock, attentively listening to Juan. He began mimicking some animal, which caused Diana to laugh hysterically as their horses stared at them.

A short time afterwards, Diana sat on Juan's upper back as she tried to reach for a pear on a branch. She managed to pluck two such fruits. She proceeded to give one to Juan. He ate one, while Diana began to chew the other while still on his back.

Later, Diana and Juan kissed as she leaned against a tree, with a slight wind blowing against her face. He attempted to take off her nun's cap, but she put her hand on his in a gentle way. She shook her head, no. Juan did not protest, and he understood the time was not right. They looked at each other and proceeded to kiss again.

Diana and Juan walked hand in hand on a grassy field facing the sun as the sun began to retire for the evening. Their horses followed.

Several nights later, Diana stood by a sanitized washbasin at the hospital, washing her hands and wearing a surgical garment. She had just finished assisting Juan with several operations. Juan entered, also wearing a surgical garment. Like Diana's, his garment had blood stains. He immediately stood next to Diana to wash his hands. He addressed her.

"This was a full day."

"You were you'll usual splendid self."

"And you likewise." He glanced at the clock on the wall. "I haven't decided where we should meet tonight?"

"How about you'll place?"

Juan stopped washing his hands, surprised by Diana's suggestion. However, Diana appeared nonchalant about her idea. Diana stopped washing her hands and reached for a towel hanging nearby.

"My place?"

"Why yes." She gave Juan a coy look as she placed the towel back on the hanger. "Unless you wish otherwise?"

"No. My place is fine."

Diana exited as he continued to wash his hands.

A look of joy then registered on his face.

Later that night, Diana was in Juan's quarters. It resembled a hotel room, with his bed and living area in the same room. A small sink and counter were off to the side. The adjoining bathroom was the only adjacent room. Diana stood by a dresser with her habit, examining a few personal items of Juan's. She picked up one of the items. A closer look revealed a Hippocratic Oath engraved on a small wooden plaque of polished wood. Juan looked at her from the edge of his bed. He was dressed in casual clothes. Diana returned the plaque to the dresser and retrieved a portrait of Juan and his mother. The photo displayed Juan at only 10 years old, with his mother, who was in her 30s.

"Was this your mother?"

"Yes."

"She was beautiful."

"Thank you."

Diana placed the portrait back on the dresser and turned toward Juan. They looked at each other with hunger in their eyes. Without saying a word, Diana removed her shoes and cap and placed them on the dresser. Juan noticed her hair for the first time, and a sensual smile came over his face. He proceeded to stand, but Diana stopped him.

"No. Please sit."

Juan was surprised by her response, but obeyed.

"I know I am taking an awful chance being here

with you and knowing what will happen. But it has to be done. Our feelings for each other, being as they are."

Juan did not respond, as he was lost in her facial beauty. She began to take off her habit and laid it on an empty chair next to the dresser. Her slim, fit body and developed breasts were more beautiful than he could have imagined. With only the necklace Juan gave her around her neck, Juan could no longer contain himself. He quickly left his bed and began to kiss her passionately. He then proceeded to kiss her face and her neck. Moving his hands on her body.

Diana's lips parted as her passion grew. Waited for this moment as she spoke softly. "How I dreamt of your physical touch."

Juan stopped and quickly disrobed as Diana looked on. He tossed his clothes and shoes on the floor. He picked her up, and they kissed. He laid her in bed with him. He lay on top of her and momentarily looked at her necklace.

"Let me take it off."

"No. Leave it on."

They kissed passionately, and he began to go down on her. Kissing her body as they began to make love.

Later, Diana and Juan lie nude next to each other as they finish their lovemaking.

Juan kissed her. "Did you feel the way you

wanted to feel?"

"More than I ever hope for."

"There was a rush all over me when I was in you, Diana."

"I felt the same. Is it always like this?"

"Only with the one you truly desire."

"Our desires speak out for each other."

Juan reached and touched the little shoe with the diamonds on her necklace. There was a twinkle in Diana's eyes as the moonlight shone on her face. "You sparkle like these diamonds. So beautiful. So clear. Every inch of your face. Your whole being. It is all I hope for in a woman. And now I have you at last."

"And you, me."

They kissed passionately and began to make love again.

The following afternoon, in downtown Pretoria, Gertrude and Elizabeth stood in front of a produce stand full of potatoes and cauliflowers, with a vendor in his 50s behind the stand. Standing nearby, Diana was humming a merry tune. Elizabeth picked up a rather large potato and showed it to Gertrude.

"This looks rather large."

"Yes. Indeed, it does."

Elizabeth handed over the potato to the vendor. Gertrude gathered several potatoes and gave them to him. He immediately placed them in a bag.

"What else?" He asked.

"Well, let's see." Gertrude began to scrutinize the cauliflowers. Diana stood before a stand full of apples, as another merchant stood behind the fruits. Diana began to hum a happy tune as the merchant looked on with a smile. Diana walked over to the peach stand and stepped up her beat. She retrieved several peaches and handed them over to the merchant. The merchant placed them in a bag. She walked back over to the apple stand in her merry mood. Gertrude and Elizabeth studied Diana.

"She has been in a merry mood since early this morning, Sister Elizabeth."

"I know. That is so nice. Maybe the climate is starting to affect her?"

"If it begins with the name of Juan. Yes. I believe it is." Gertrude turned to Diana. "Why were you so late coming to bed last night?"

"Oh! We had an emergency. The surgery took us longer than expected."

"When you refer to we. You are referring to Dr. Sanchez and yourself?"

"I am his assistant."

"She has a point, Sister Gertrude. "

Gertrude said nothing as she studied Diana for a moment. Diana then began humming to herself again and handed some apples to the merchant for purchase. Gertrude turned to Elizabeth.

"Sister Helen thinks otherwise."

"You know Sister Helen. She doesn't trust anyone."

"Hmm...."

A short time afterwards, Diana, Gertrude, and Elizabeth walked down a street carrying their produce bags. Diana said hello to almost everyone she passed. The nuns suddenly came across several children standing against a building, all playing with each other. Diana approached them, as Gertrude and Elizabeth looked on.

"Here, children. I have a treat for you all." She handed each of them a peach from her bag. "Now you children be good. And stay out of trouble."

They replied in unison. "We will, Sister."

"Good little ones."

Diana padded each one of them on the head. A smile radiates on each of their faces. Diana left the children as they began to bite on their peaches. Gertrude and Elizabeth followed close behind.

Gertrude interjected. "You sure have been rather jovial today."

"Yes, Sister. You have."

"We should be this way every day."

"That would be wonderful if we could. Right, Sister Gertrude?"

"Why yes indeed."

Diana began to sign as she moved about.

"We should all try to be happy
At least a little each day
All it takes is just a little each day
Yes, we should be happy a little each day

I can show you unhappy people
With their sad and unhappy faces
But show a little happiness
And their frowns will turn into smiles."

Suddenly, the nuns came across a horse-driven carriage standing by a street curve. However, the carriage was empty. Diana reached into her bag and pulled out an apple. She placed the apple near the horse's mouth. Gertrude and Elizabeth look on.

Gertrude's jaw dropped. "Not the horse?"

"Why, Sister Gertrude. Horses have to eat, too. Come on, horsy. Take a bite."

Elizabeth giggled at this. The horse studied Diana briefly, and she smiled back at the horse. The horse decided to take a bite.

"That's right. It's all yours."

The horse took another bite and began to finish the apple.

Gertrude was somewhat surprised. "The horse was rather hungry."

Elizebeth injected, "She sure was."

"It's a mare," Diana replied.

Elizebeth covered her mouth. "Oh!"

Diana continued to sing.

"Everyone deserves to smile
All it takes is a little sunlight
Shining on their faces
And happiness can make it happen."

Diana smiled at the nuns. "Come on, Sisters. Show me your smiles."

A small crowd gathered around the nuns. It made Gertrude feel uncomfortable.

"Sister Diana. I believe we should carry on."

Diana waved at the horse. "Bye, horsy." She gently kissed the horse's cheeks as he continued to chew on the apple thoroughly. The nuns then proceeded to walk on as the crowd applauded Diana.

Gertrude turned to Elizabeth. "Well. Whatever she has, I hope it's contagious."

"Yes." Elizabeth beam.

Diana said bye to the people they walked past, and they smiled back at her.

CHAPTER 8 – TWISTED FATE

A month had passed, and Juan and Diana saw each other when they could. Outside of the hospital, of course. However, it was no longer an easy task. People around them began to talk and gossip about Diana and Juan. So, Diana and Juan needed to be discreet in their comings and goings. Diana frequently flirted with Juan, and their lively conversations in the hospital hallways were a common occurrence. Their eyes, always dancing at each other, made it obvious that something else was happening between them than just taking care of the patients. However, the suggestion of meeting alone again at Juan's quarters was out of the question. Not that they did not want to. Their sensual passion was very much alive for each other. It was just too risky. Not just for Diana, but also for Juan. He was afraid he could lose his medical license over their affair. And he worked too hard to become a medical doctor.

A few of the nuns were beginning to suspect the same, especially Helen, who always distrusted Diana. She believed Diana's heart was not in the right place and tried to convince Dorothy privately that Diana should not be allowed to take her vows when they returned to Ireland. However, Dorothy waved Helen off and told her to keep her opinions about Diana to herself. Ruth was also on the receiving end of some of the gossip, but dismissed it as pure folly.

Diana soon realized she must leave the sisterhood to continue her relationship with Juan. She felt she could no longer play the charade of creating a respectable appearance with the sisters while at the same time having a sexual relationship with the man she desired to spend the rest of her life with. Something had to give. Either Juan or she would have to take their relationship to the next level and risk it all. But who?

Several days later, Ruth unexpectedly received an urgent request from a field hospital and decided to give the task to Juan. Assigning Juan away from the hospital might cease the rumormongering concerning Diana and Juan at the hospital. Juan was attending to a patient when Ruth approached him.

"Juan. Medical Staff requests your assistance at the field hospital near Doornkop."

"Doornkop? There are physicians over there."

"One of the surgeons became ill." She took a deep breath. "The British are making their way to Johannesburg. The commandos will try to stop them at Doornkop."

"So, there will be a battle there?"

"It appears so."

Juan gave a sad, faraway stare. "I see."

"Can I tell the staff they can count on you? It will only be for a week."

Juan reluctantly nodded.

"Good." She smiled at Juan and left.

Juan was lost in thought.

Later that night at the hospital, Juan was at his desk in his small office. He had just finished writing a letter as he sat behind his desk. James, a 12-year-old African boy, looked on. Juan folded the letter and handed it to him.

"Now, James. You know what to do? Don't you?"

"Yes. Doctor. I am supposed to give this letter to Sister Diana when she is alone."

"And if you cannot find her?"

"I am supposed to leave it at her quarters."

"That is correct."

"How come you will not give it to her?"

"I have to leave now, while it is still dark. I will not have the time to say goodbye to her properly."

"Are you going to marry her?"

"James, for God's sake! She is a nun."

"You did not answer my question."

Juan took a deep breath. "Is it that obvious?"

James responded with a big grin on his face.

"Look, when I come back. I will have a present for you."

"Really!"

"Yes. Now run alone."

"Okay."
James quickly left, as Juan smiled at him.

Later, James decided to enter the boarding house carrying the letter, but could not find anyone. Diana and Elizabeth's room had an open window above their beds. Bright moonlight entered the room. Above the window, James viewed a portrait of the Virgin Mary. Besides the bed was a dresser with a mirror attached. On the right corner of the mirror was Elizabeth's name tag, and on the left corner was Diana's name. After looking at the room momentarily, James walked over to the dresser. He decided to lay the letter on the edge of the dresser. He exited the room. Suddenly, a strong breeze entered from the open window and knocked the letter to the floor. Another strong breeze pushed the letter underneath Diana's bed.

Later that night, Diana entered Juan's office in the hospital. Diana stood in the office and stared at an empty desk. Diana walked toward it and looked for anything that would explain his whereabouts. Suddenly, Ruth walked in.
"Can I help you with anything, Diana?"
"I was looking for Dr. Sanchez?"
"The doctor is off to Doornkop."
"Doornkop?"
"General Botha's men badly need a surgeon."
"No one told me."

"Well, now you know. Come along."

Diana left the office with Ruth. Diana and Ruth stood outside Juan's office.

"How long will he be gone?"

"No more than a week depending on the outcome."

"I don't understand?"

"There is expected to be some heavy fighting coming soon. And one of the few physicians came down with a bad case of pneumonia."

Diana did not say anything, as melancholy was written all over her face.

"Don't worry, my child. He will return safe and sound. Now, I need you to assist Doctor Roos in surgery."

Diana did not respond, as she was lost in thought.

"Diana?"

"Yes, ma'am. I will be there."

"Good."

Ruth walked away, leaving Diana alone. Diana's mind called for him.

"My God be with you, my love."

Several days later, in late May, the battle of Doornkop had begun. Under General Field Marshal Earl Roberts, the British led their army of over 20,000 men to take Johannesburg and then made their thrust to the capital city of Pretoria. The

Boers had lost to Roberts in a significant battle at Paardeberg earlier in the year. Roberts no longer received much resistance until he reached the Klipriversberg range, where Doornkop lay along with over 2,000 waiting Boer commandoes. Once the British overran Doornkop, Johannesburg would be for their taking. Robert used two of his subordinate generals, French and Hamilton, to move their forces west of Johannesburg. At the same time, he deployed his other subordinate generals, Tucker and Pole-Carew, along the rail lines east of Johannesburg.

On this first day, the British and the Boers traded artillery fire. The British had 30 artillery pieces, while the Boers had their Long Tom Gun, a 155 mm Creusot siege gun.

On the following morning, the British tried to advance up the ridge under General French with mounted cavalry, but they were fired upon by Boer sharpshooters who were encamped behind large rocks on the ridge in Doornkop. Looking down on them, the Boer commandos saw the British cavalry mounted on their horses as easy targets.

French decided to withdraw his troops, and Hamilton's men took over the charge with two infantry brigades. They were the Gordan Highlanders. The Imperial Volunteers from London and the Royal Canadian Regiment also joined the fight. They came in waves. The Boer waited until the British came closer, setting fire to the grassland ahead of Hamilton's men to slow them down. The Boers then fired down on the British. Volley after volley hit the British hard, as men fell all around. But the British returned their rifle fire with their Lee-Enfield rifles, as the Boers kept their defensive position. The British Lee-Enfield bolt-action rifle held a 10-round detachable magazine.

The Boers sent some men under Boer General Koos de la Rey to meet the other British threat from General Tucker and Pole-Carew, who were moving their men along the rail lines. Their objective was to outflank the Boer commanders and prevent them from retreating to Pretoria.

Meanwhile, Boer General Louis Botha rode his horse with several other officers. He stopped his horse a short distance above the Boer sharpshooter's firing line. He decided to survey the British positions with his field glasses. Likewise, his aides stopped, awaiting the General's next orders. British rifle fire kicked up dirt near the general. But Botha did not flinch as he continued to scan the British. Suddenly, a field-cornet rider came and stopped his horse by Botha.

"What is it, Field-Cornet?"

"Our artillery officer is severely wounded in the chest, General Botha."

"Well, take him to the field hospital."

CHAPTER 8 – TWISTED FATE

"We have no wagons to spare."

"Well, don't just sit there. Round up some Kakebeenwaens from the farmers nearby. Or the wounded will die on the field."

Field-Cornet saluted Botha. "Yes, General."

Field-Cornet was about to ride away when Botha called for him. "Wait! Bring back a surgeon to attend to our artillery officer before he bleeds to death."

"Yes. General." Field-Cornet gallops away.

"Come on. I need a better view." General Botha rode to another position on the battlefield as his aids followed close behind.

Juan was in a makeshift field hospital near the battlefield. He was finishing the stitching of a wounded Boer soldier on a rough-and-ready table with a male nurse assisting. Juan's operating garments were soaked with blood. A Boer soldier cried nearby as his leg was being amputated. Suddenly, the field-cornet rushed in. Juan looked up and addressed him.

"Yes."

General Botha has called upon you to assist with our severely wounded artillery officer.

"Where is he?"

"Near the front line."

"Why is he not here?"

"We have no more wagons."

Juan took a deep breath. "All right. Where is he wounded?"

"In the chest area. Near his heart."

Juan turned to the male nurse as he continued sewing the patient.

"I shall be back shortly. Finish with him. There are only a few stitches left." Juan handed the male nurse the swing instruments. Juan left with the field-cornet.

Juan and the field cornet rode on their horses as they galloped to the site of the wounded artillery officer. Attached to Juan's saddle was his medical bag. Juan heard rifle fire, barely missing them. Suddenly, the horse carrying Juan threw him off his saddle. The field cornet stopped his horse and quickly dismounted to assist Juan, who lay on the ground.

"Are you all right?"

Juan managed to stand. "A few bumps. But I'm fine."

"Good sir."

"Their rifle fire can be frightening. Are you not afraid of being hit?"

"They come close. But the British are not always good shots."

Without saying another word, Juan and the field-cornet reached their saddles.

"Come, doctor. We are almost there."

"Well, let's proceed."

The field-cornet began to gallop away. Juan was about to do the same when, unexpectedly, a British sharpshooter landed a bullet directly at Juan. Juan fell to the ground and appeared lifeless.

CHAPTER 8 – TWISTED FATE

Several days later, the nuns dressed in their black habits, and others gathered in a simple grave site to bury Juan at the local Pretoria cemetery. Everyone stood beside the site, tossing a handful of dirt on top of the casket as it was being lowered. This included Diana, who was grieving. She also clung to the necklace Juan gave her. The other nuns saw the necklace and looked at each other in surprise. They did not recognize the jewelry before.

Later that night, a small group gathered after Juan's funeral at the hospital chapel. The group included the nuns and a few hospital staff members, including Ruth. Against a wall was a small table where coffee was being served. Dorothy sat behind the piano as she began to play slow, melancholic music.

Adeline approached Ruth. "The British will be entering Pretoria soon. What will become of the hospital?"

Ruth sipped her coffee. "I would not worry too much."

"Why, may I ask?"

"The British will need this facility to treat their wounded. Most medical staff will be required to work for their new masters." She took another sip. She gave Adeline a look of disgust. "This war makes me sick." She then walked away.

Meanwhile, Gertrude and Helen engaged in their chit-chat as they drank their coffee.

Helen narrowed her eyes and slightly raised her eyebrows at Gertrude. "I told you she was having an affair with that doctor."

"We do not know that for sure."

"Who else would have given that necklace? You saw how she reacted at the funeral."

Gertrude noticed a hospital employee. "Oh. I see someone I must talk to."

Helen persisted. "We should take some action?"

Gertrude ignored her as she walked away.

Meanwhile, outside the chapel, a lonely Diana leaned against the wall as the night sky was full of bright stars. Tears were falling from her eyes as she clung to the necklace. She heard the music Dorothy was playing on the piano. Her face said it all. She cried and looked up at the stars as the nightly light descended on her.

"Oh... I'm so confused. So very confused. Why, dear Lord? Why? I love him so much. Was it because I was not supposed to have loved another as I did for Juan? But if it was wrong, then tell me. Give me a sign. You should not have let him die. No!" For a moment, she appeared lost in thought. She then began to sing as if singing to the Lord.

> "Is it wrong to love another
> To love what you can touch
> To be happy for one so true
> Is it wrong to want that love
>
> I want to find that love

To love this special someone
Find this one before it's too late
Isn't that what I should be living for

Should I run if I found this love
Should I hide what I feel
Or do I just never fall in love
I need to hear it from you

If I am not allowed to find this love
This love with someone new
Then, I will stay devoted to you
And ask nothing more from you

But if I can find this love
To have him close to me
I shall never let him go
Is that what I should do

Should I run if I found this love
Should I hide what I feel
Or do I never fall in love
I need to hear it from you

For he is just a man
He is not like you
So, I will stay beholden to you
For that is all I can offer to you."

Diana then wiped her tears as she covered her face with her hands. She still clung to the necklace as she continued to cry. Dorothy's music came to an end.

Diana was alone in her quarters the following day

at the boarding house. She had changed the sheets on her bed. However, a sad look was painted on her face because of Juan's death. The window was open, and sunlight entered the room. She stopped and walked over to the dresser to retrieve a clean pillowcase. She opened a drawer and pulled out the linen. However, she accidentally dropped the pillowcase, falling to the floor. She went over and picked up the linen. However, in doing so, she discovered the letter Juan had written underneath her bed. She picked up the letter and unfolded it. She was surprised to realize the letter was from him. She sat at the edge of the bed to read the letter to herself.

> *"My love, if you read this, I will be in Doornkop attending to the wounded the best I can. When I return in a week, I will have my arms around you again. I want you to consider marrying me. I know of your situation. But you must have a change of heart about your Sisterhood. The Lord, whoever or whatever it is, is not always easy to understand. And there is no sure way we can fully understand this entity. This entity we call God."*

Diana stopped reading the letter, lost in thought, contemplating Juan's message. She then continued with the letter.

> *"But your marriage to me will not alter your faith. It will not change*

your spiritual values. I believe it will make it that much stronger. Being together. Raising a family. I know you have thought about this many times. So, change your heart to match mine. We can both follow your faith together, as husband and wife. I will see you soon. From your love. Juan."

Finished with the letter, she began to cry.

CHAPTER 9 - CHANGING OF THE GUARD

On June 05, 1900, the British army marched into Pretoria by the thousands. Various people lined the street to observe them. The crowd did not show much emotion on their arrival, as the British marched peacefully but triumphantly. Two Boer women, Maria and Johanna, in their thirties, observe the fanfare as they converse. They were dressed in their Sunday best.

Maria smiled as she placed a hand over her eyes for shade. "Now that the British have Johannesburg and Pretoria, we will finally see an end to this short war."

"Don't count too much on that. They still haven't caught General Botha."

"General Botha cannot do a damn thing, Johanna."

"Hope you are right."

"About Botha?"

"About the war being close to an end."

Maria was all smiles. "Yes. It is finished."

The British continued to march victoriously through the downtown streets.

It was now October 1900, and the war with the Boers was still strong. The British military believed that capturing the capital cities of Bloemfontein and Pretoria would quickly bring the war to a swift end. But it did not. Instead, the Boer commandoes took to the hills and launched a bitter guerrilla campaign against the British Army. Led by such generals as Louis Botha and Christiaan de Wet. This type of warfare was not familiar to the British. To make matters worse, the commandos picked which areas to attack based on their familiarity with the land and received aid from their families and friends, mostly Dutch.

Field Marshal Roberts realized his difficulty, changed tactics, and took the war to the citizens. This meant controversial methods were employed, such as destroying civilian farms. He also implemented concentration camps, sending women and children to military-style camps as prisoners after the British military burned down their farms and homes, since there was no other place for them to go. However, Roberts left his post after laying out his controversial methods and passed the baton to General Herbert Kitchener in November 1900, who was quickly promoted to Lieutenant General.

Needless to say, Kitchener continued with the strategies Roberts had laid out and expanded them to force the Boer commandos to surrender. The concentration camps, being the most controversial, were nothing new. They have been used before, but on a limited scale. The British military took the camps to a new level, targeting a whole nation systematically, which resulted in entire regions being depopulated. This was never done before, and this type of method would not be seen again until future wars by other nations. As a result, thousands of women and children would die in Boer and Black African camps.

It was February 25, 1901, and from the skyline, one saw the Tower of London, Tower Bridge, and the Clock Tower. The Houses of Parliament, consisting of a group of buildings of the House of Commons and House of Lords along the banks of the River Thames, were in full view.

Parliament was in full session in the Common Chamber inside the House of Commons. The Commons were in a hot debate over the situation in South Africa. Since the war has continued, it has caused intense crises in Great Britain. The party representing the Government sat on one side, which included Prime Minister Lord Salisbury and his cabinet.

Meanwhile, the Opposition party sat directly on the other side. Lord Salisbury and his cabinet sat on the front bench nearest the chamber's center. The Speaker of the House, presiding over the session, banged his gavel to call for order as both parties yelled at each other. Finally, quiet was within reach.

The Speaker continued. "Thank you. The chair reorganizes the distinguish member from Ireland, John Dillon."

Dillon quickly stood. "Thank you, Mr. Speaker." He addressed the chamber. "The Secretary of State for the Colonies, in the speech which he delivered on Monday night, which was characterized by an almost ferocious bitterness, hurled across the floor of this House the epithet "Pro-Boer" as a term of reproach to honorable Members sitting on this side of the House. So far as I am concerned, and the other Members who sit on these benches, the Secretary for the Colonies is welcome to call us pro-Boers."

Government members shout from the other side. "So, you are."

Dillion continued. "I am a pro-Boer because during the last two years, I have made a careful study of the history of these people."

Laughter from the members representing the Government.

Dillion continued. "I do not suppose that honorable members opposite who laugh have taken the slightest interest in that history, and yet it is one of the most interesting that they could find. I am convinced from the study that they have been deeply wronged for many generations by the Government of England, that they are now fighting for freedom against enormous odds, and that they are two small States fighting for their national existence against the cruel and unprovoked aggression of an Empire which is too large already to be wholesome."

He paused, and then continued. "We Irish members, and the Irish people for whom we speak, deeply sympathize with these two small States, who are fighting the most glorious and gallant fight which modern history has any record of, and we think it is a magnificent thing in these modern days that there exist men who are willing to risk everything and lose all for an ideal, and for liberty."

Members of the Opposition party sitting on Dillon's side momentarily cheer in agreement.

Dillon continued. "For these reasons, we are not ashamed to be called pro-Boers. The other night, the Secretary of State for the Colonies threw a challenge across the floor of this House, and I am glad that, speaking for the Irish party on this occasion. I am able to say that there is a party in this House who are not afraid to bring this matter to an issue."

Members of the Opposition party sitting on Dillon's side momentarily cheer in agreement.

Dillon continued. "The Amendment which I propose to submit to the judgment of this House affirms two propositions: First, that the breaches of the usages of war by the British, which have been going on for many months in South Africa, should be taken immediately to put stop to; and second, that steps should be taken immediately to put an end to this miserable and scandalous war."

Dillon again paused as his party cheered his remarks, and the Government party jeered back at the Opposition.

A month has passed since the Parliament debate, and the sky was blue on another pleasant day at Bloemfontein camp. Various tents were shaped like teepees, surrounded by barbed wire fences about five meters high. The camp covered about ten acres, in which around 3,500 Boer women and children were prisoners of war. The tents were designed to hold approximately six inhabitants. But in some cases, the number per tent exceeded this, depending on the size of each family. The conditions at the camps were horrible. Officially, the British informed the international press that these were volunteer camps, but in actuality, they were concentration camps.

Children of all ages play around the tents at Bloemfontein as their mothers wash their clothes on various pools of water on the ground left by the rain the night before, since the camp, like the others, had no adequate water system.

About ten girls sat on damp logs, pulling their

dresses up as they urinated. In between the logs was a small ditch, which served as a latrine.

Some children lie outside their tents, as old crumpled newspapers serve as their protection against the muddy ground. They were staring into the blue sky, lost in thought. They also appeared to be emaciated children as their limbs were thin, with protruding bones, sunken eyes, dry skin, their hair thinning, and bloated stomachs. Malnutrition ran rampant in the camps.

A dozen or so open-drawn wagons left off new Boer arrivals. Each wagon was crammed with about thirty women and children. They exit the wagon like cattle, as a small group of British soldiers supervise their arrival.

The Boers wore traditional clothes and only carried a few personal items. However, one Boer woman refused to leave the wagon. British Corporal Harris took action, pulling her off the wagon. This caused her to land on the muddy ground, and her clothes became mud-covered. Two other British corporals, Jones and Woodson, laughed at this. The woman stood and kicked Harris in the leg, thus causing his clean uniform pants to be marked with mud stains. Harris was now very angry and shoved the woman hard. She fell to the ground again, causing more laughter from the corporals. Harris now aimed his rifle at the woman on the muddy ground. She was also angry at Harris, as her face was rage-filled.

"If you dare to strike me one more time. I swear I'll shoot you."

Jones chuckled. "Go ahead and shoot her. It will make my day."

Woodson nodded his head. "Just put her out of her misery."

Harris barked his order. "Now stand up, you bitch!"

She stood up, as her clothes were soaked with mud.

"Now get back with the others."

"You British pig!"

The soldiers laugh.

"I believe you are the pig here, "Harris replied. "Now, hurry up. Hurry up."

The soldiers laughed again. The Boer women and children stood in front of the wagons. Mitchell, a British sergeant nicknamed Mitch, appeared, holding a black baton. The women and children stared at him with fright.

He stared back at them, not one too happy. "Come on, you, Burghers. Let's form a straight line here. Or do I have to say it in Dutch?"

Suddenly, the Boer women and children began to form a straight line in front of the wagons. The sergeant was now satisfied.

He continued. "This is where you all will be until this war is finally terminated. Medical treatment and whatever else you need to survive will be at the camp." His eyes narrowed, and his lips curled. "You are to do what we say, and when we say it. Anyone trying to leave this camp will be shot. And I mean anyone."

A Boer woman in her 20s spoke out. "When will this war end?"

The sergeant walked over to her in an irritated fashion. "When you'll damn fathers, husbands, boyfriends, brothers, any other damn Boer soldiers decide to stop their fighting." He walked closer. His face was only inches from hers. "Do I make myself clear?"

She began to sob. "Yes."

He replied with a grin. "Good." He then turned and faced Jones. "Now, everyone looked at Corporal Jones."

Jones momentarily raised his hand.

"He will assign you to your new homes. You could call it your home away from home."

The British soldiers laughed.

Jones then motioned to the Boer women and children. "Follow me, burglars."

Jones began to walk away as the women and children crowded around him. Several of the soldiers grab a few of the women rather harshly.

Harris addressed one of the women. "Did you not hear that everyone was to form a line? Now go back?" Harris yanked her by the arm and pushed her aside.

Several soldiers did the same to the other women. The women moved behind everyone else. Several of the children followed the women since they were their mothers.

Woodson addressed the group. "And that goes for the rest of you blooming Boer."

The women and children formed a long line as they followed Jones. Satisfied, Sergeant Mitchell left.

The following day, the camp's makeshift hospital was receiving new patients. The building had walls and a roof made of cheap tin. Some one hundred patients, women and children, lay in cots. White linen covered the cots, and most patients appeared to have a bad case of malnutrition.

Diana decided to work at the camp hospital. She could have stayed at Volks Hospital when the British took over Pretoria, but she wanted to leave, break away from Pretoria as far as she could, and still help those in need. Volks reminded her of the emotional turmoil she was going through with Juan's death and the love she wanted to marry. There were also the constant rumors flowing around at the hospital that she was romantically linked to him, and the nuns were questioning her devotion to the sisterhood.

The other nuns decided to leave for Ireland. They had seen enough of the war and no longer had the desire to stay. The British military gave the nuns safe passage back to their country. However, Diana needed permission to stay in South Africa. To her surprise, Mother Theresa wired her, giving her permission, provided her services were still required. The Red Cross, as well as the British military, indicated they could use her. So, Diana requested to work somewhere else. Ruth hated to see her go. She grew fond of her, and she gained valuable nursing skills.

The British medical staff then transferred her to the Bloemfontein camp by train, where she was most needed. She was allowed to wear her white novitiate habit but was ordered to return the black one to Dorothy, since the nuns had left, and she was not quite yet a nun until she took her official vows in Ireland, which now had to wait. So, she sat on the train wearing her white habit and contemplating on recent events that had unfolded in her life. She closed her eyes and recalled Mother Theresa ordering her to travel to South Africa to provide medical aid. She remembered the first time she laid eyes on Juan in the train. She then reflected on Helen accusing her in front of the other nuns of having an affair with Juan as they finished their shopping at a local store. She had an image of her and Juan kissing as they began to make love in his quarters. The letter Juan wrote to her proposing marriage. She then opened her eyes and stared aimlessly out the window, as the train continued on its journey.

Wearing her white novitiate habit, Diana attended to one of the patients covered by a thin blanket at the camp. It was a twelve-year-old Dutch boy named Johnny. Diana was taking his temperature with a thermometer. She examined the instrument, and dread came over her face. The boy looked at her with his sick eyes.

"Oh dear." She touched his forehead. "Are you still having chills?"

"Yes."

"I'll be back." Diana quickly left with the thermometer.

An English doctor named Charles Rhodes, in his 50s, was conversing with Ann, an English nurse in her late 30s. They both appeared to be in the middle of a cheerful discussion.

"I mean, can you picture the look on his face?"

Ann was all smiles. "I can just imagine Charles."

They both laugh.

"And his wife was standing right there."

Ann covered her mouth. "Oh, my word!"

They laugh again. Diana appeared and interpreted their conversation.

"Doctor Rhodes."

"Yes, Diana."

"I was examining a little boy just a minute ago, and I believe he is coming down with malaria."

"Which boy?"

"Johnny."

"Johnny... Johnny. Oh yes. I remember the little fellow. Well. I saw him the other day, and I did not come to that conclusion."

"Examine him now."

"I'm rather busy."

"Did you examine his chest? Check his

temperature?"

"Dear. Are you telling me how to do my job?"

"This lad is very sick!"

"Look around you. Everyone is sick. This is a hospital. Is it not?"

Ann giggled at Charles's remark.

"Can I give him quinine?"

"You may certainly not."

"He needs it, doctor!"

"We ran out of quinine."

Diana was not backing down. "I thought you put in a requisition for some last week."

"Why yes, I did... Didn't I?"

Ann shrugged her shoulders at her. "You are supposed to be a nun. Why don't you pray for him?"

Diana looked at Charles and Ann with contempt and walked away. Charles and Ann followed her with their eyes.

"She is going to be trouble, Charles."

"Yes. I can see that."

Diana walked back towards Johnny. His eyes were closed as he fell asleep. Diana placed her hand over his forehead and closed her eyes. She prayed in silence for a few moments. She opened her eyes and kissed his forehead.

She spoke to him softly. "Sleep, little one."

She left and decided to walk to check on another patient. In doing so, she came across two African children carrying bedpans. The African boy's name was Shaka, age 10, and his little sister was named Elandria, age 7. They were barefoot.

Diana greeted, "Hello. But I do not recall seeing both of you before."

Shaka and Elandria did not say a word while holding the pans.

"Do you both know any English?"

Shaka replied, as Elandria usually stayed quiet. "Yes. We both know the language. Ma'am."

"What are your names?"

"My name is Shaka, and she is my sister. Her name is Elandria. We are both going to the latrine."

"You both are new here."

"Yes, ma'am."

"Where are both of you from?"

"The African camp nearby. Both parents died there."

"I am so sorry, children."

"They do not allow anyone from our village in the Boer Camp. But the English said for us to work here."

"Is your camp like this one?"

Elandria finally spoke. "Yes."

Shaka replied. "Except we have no doctors."

"No doctor! Are you sure?"

Shaka nodded his head. "Yes, ma'am."

"That cannot be right."

Shaka felt uneasy. "We have to go, ma'am."

"Shaka. You can call me Diana. And that goes for you to Elandria."

Skaka and Elandria replied in unison. "Yes, Diana."

Shaka decided to ask a question. "Why are you dressed like this?"

"I am a Nun. Well ...actually a novitiate until I receive my vows."

Shaka and Elandria replied with blank stares.

"I represent a sisterhood of a Christian denomination. One of these days, I will teach you about it."

Elandria managed to smile. "Okay."

Shaka and Elandria then quickly left, as Diana smiled at them.

The following day at the camp, various Boer women and children stood in line holding ration cards and small wooden bowls, which led to a long-serving mess table. Near the table stood two British soldiers who kept an eye on the Boers. Two male cooks served the food. A Boer woman reached the table and handed her ration card to Fred, who appeared to be in his 20s. He placed the card in a wooden box. He scooped some gooey rice from a large pot on the table and put it in her wooden bowl. He handed it to the other cook, Ralph, who was in his 40s. Ralph then placed some meat in it. The beef appeared chilled, as some ice was in it. Next in line was Emma and her seven-year-old son. She held a bowl with her portion and handed Fred her son's empty bowl.

"Where's your card?"

"It's for my son. I was here earlier. But I threw my son's food away because worms were in his rice."

"I suppose you want me to refill your boy's bowl?"

"Why yes."

Ralph overheard the conversation and intervened. "There are no worms in this here rice. Can't you see she's lying so she can have an extra helping."

"That's not so!"

Ralph continued. "You know the rules. Only one serving. I suggest you give your boy your share."

"I will not."

"Now look here, Missy. I don't want any trouble from you."

"I tell you, I saw maggots!"

"If you open your mouth one more time, I'll call the guards."

Emma looked at Ralph with a dreadful stare. She decided to leave, holding the boy's hand as the cooks continued serving the food. Emma walked a short distance and stopped. Although still angry, she gave her food to her son, who immediately ate it.

The next day, in one of the many tents, there were two sets of families: seven Boer women and children in somewhat cramped conditions. The ground was nothing but soil since the British did not provide any floor covering for the Boers. The occupants were Sara Tielman, age forty-three, with her children Paul, age thirteen, and her daughter Mary, who just turned twelve. The other family was Deborah Klopper, who was thirty-nine, and her three children, Samuel, the oldest at thirteen, Joseph, who was ten, and Margaret, who was eight. Their clothes were rather tattered and dirty. Joseph was asleep and appeared to be emaciated.

Suddenly, Sergeant Major Reynolds and Second Corporal Nicholson entered the tent to everyone's surprise. They carried a traveling chest. They observed the occupants and decided to lay the chest down.

Reynolds waved Diana in. "Sister Diana. You may enter."

Diana entered, wearing her white habit to the amazement of the Boer occupants.

Nicholson displayed a sad look. "I am sorry, Sister."

"No. It's quite alright."

Reynolds attempted to put on a happy face. "Things will patch up with the good doctor. Besides, the hospital would not be the same without you."

Nicholson echoed the sentiment. "Yes, Sister. He's the one who should be in here."

Reynolds tensed up. "Maybe they will replace the blooming bastard!" Realizing his aggressive tone in front of the children, apologized. "Sorry,

Sister."

"Don't worry. Everything will turn out fine. Thank you both for carrying my belongings."

Nicholson lights up a smile. "You are quite welcome, Sister."

Both soldiers smiled at Diana as they left. Everyone in the tent was bewildered by Diana's presence, especially the children.

Margaret said, "Gee. We now have a sister living with us."

Samuel said with sincerity. "Maybe she will perform a miracle for us."

His mother, Deborah, was not thrilled. "Hush, Samuel!"

"That's quite all right. And by the way. Everyone can call me Diana."

Deborah gave Diana a stern look. "You'll be Irish. Aren't you?"

"Yes."

"Hmm. Well, as long as you're not English. That's fine with me."

Sara displayed a smile. "Come, please sit."

"Thank you." Diana proceeded to sit in front of Deborah and Margaret. "I see we have a full house here."

Sara replied. "Each tent is to be for a family. But they are now assigning two families per tent because they are running low on shelters. Let me introduce myself. My name is Sara Tielman, and these are my children. Paul and Mary. Paul and Mary say hello to Diana."

Paul replied first. "Hello."

Mary was next, "Glad to meet you, Sister. I-I-I mean Diana."

"It's a pleasure to meet you both."

Diana addressed Sara. "How old are your children?"

"Paul is thirteen, while Mary is twelve."

Diana turned to Deborah and Margaret. "And what is your name, little darling?"

"My name is Margaret. And I turned eight."

Diana then turned and smiled at Deborah. "She's adorable."

"My name is Deborah Klopper." Deborah turned to her other children. "And these are my other children, Samuel and Joseph. Samuel is twelve, while Joseph, who's asleep, is ten."

Samuel was all smiles. "Hello."

"They are all darlings." Diana studied Joseph for a moment. "He is not doing too well, Mom."

"No. I am afraid not."

"Malnutrition is hitting the camp very hard."

Mary changed the subject. "Are you from Ireland?"

"Why, yes, I am."

Paul was also curious. "How long have you been a nun?"

"Well, actually, I'm not a nun yet."

Mary raised her hand.

"Yes, Mary."

"Shouldn't you wear a black habit? "

"I have to take my vows first. Until I do, I wear white. I did have a black habit when I arrived. But I had to return it to the sisters who left for Ireland."

Margaret looked confused. "Vows?"

"Yes. Acceptance into the sisterhood. Technically, I am only a novitiate. Although I do perform many duties a nun does."

Samual was impressed. "Wow!"

Diana turned to the mothers. "Do the children sleep often?"

Sara answered. "Not at first. But they have been napping more often the last several weeks."

Diana expressed a worried look on her face. "I see."

"What's wrong?" Deborah said.

"You see, a child's body becomes weak due to malnutrition. This causes the child to sleep more often. Have the children started to have cramps or diarrhea?"

"My Mary has."

"And my son, Joseph."

Diana gently pinched Joseph's cheeks. "He's so adorable."

Deborah returned Diana's compliment with a bright smile.

"Yes. With the events as they are now. More

and more children have very little resistance to diseases and…"

Samuel interrupted. "Me and Margaret were playing scissors. Do you want to play?"

"Samuel! Do not speak unless you are spoken to!"

"I'm afraid, Samuel, I have to pass up now. Maybe tomorrow."

"How long will we continue living this way?"

"Unfortunately, Deborah, I do not have an answer. I know something must be done rather quickly, or there will be many more fatalities."

Deborah said, "You would think they are trying to kill us all by forcing us to live in these conditions."

"I cannot say. But at the hospital, if you want to call it that. More and more children are breaking out with the measles."

Sara interjected. "Aren't the doctors doing anything?"

"There is only one doctor, and his medical ethics are appalling. Many children with measles will not produce enough antibodies to fight the infection."

"Was it the doctor who put you with us?"

"Yes, Sara. He threatens to have me shot if I continue complaining about the awful conditions at the hospital. But I don't think everyone in England knows about these awful conditions."

Deborah squinted, "What are you saying?"

"The military has not been truthful about its affairs with the public at home."

"Oh dear!" Sara said.

"But being here gives me solace that I will be treated no differently than anyone else in this camp."

Paul gasped. "So, you will be in here for good?"

Mary bellowed, "Have you not been listening?"

Diana smiled, "Yes, Paul. Is that all right?"

Paul smiled ear to ear, "Yaw!"

Suddenly, Joseph awoke from their sleep. As soon as his eyes opened, he looked up at Diana with surprise.

"Hello. You must be Joseph?"

He did not say a word as he stared at Diana in amazement.

"Did you have a pleasant sleep?"

Joseph responded by nodding his head as Diana smiled back.

"Joseph! Answer her," his mother said.

"Yes, ma'am."

"No, honey. Call her Diana."

"Diana," Joseph said softly.

To bring up everyone's spirits, Diana had an idea. "I am sure one of you knows a song?"

Margaret was quick with an answer. "Roll, Roll, Roll Your Boat."

Diana nodded, "I like that song."

Diana addressed the mothers. "Is it all right if the children can sing?"

"Yes. By all means," Sara explained.

Deborah shrugs her shoulders. "Yaw. Why not?"

"Good. Now, does everyone know the song?"

All the children responded by saying yes, except for Samuel.

Diana addressed Samuel, "You do not know Roll, Roll, Roll Your Boat?"

"No."

Margaret gasped. "Yes, you do, you liar!"

"How often have I told you not to call your brother a liar?"

"Sorry, Mom."

Diana intervened, "If you do not. Just follow along. Now the girls will sing the first verse, and the boys will sing the second."

The children smiled as they waited in anticipation. Diana began to sing, and the girls joined in.

"Roll, roll, roll your boat.
Gently down the stream."

Diana looked at the boys as she continued singing.

"Merrily, merrily, merrily, merrily.
Life is but a dream."

But the boys did not sing, as they stared at Diana. "Boys. Let's hear it." Diana sang again as the boys joined in.

"Merrily, merrily, merrily, merrily.

Life is but a dream."

"Good boys. Now that we have it. Shall we continue?"

Diana and the girls began to sing again.

"Roll, roll, roll your boat.

Gently down the stream."

Now it was Diana's and the boy's turn to sing.

"Merrily, merrily, merrily, merrily.

Life is but a dream."

Diana continued to lead the children as they cheerily sang in harmony. The mothers smiled at the lively event.

Their voices carried over and could be heard from outside their tent among the sea of tents. Some children who were walking by decided to stop to listen to their singing.

Several weeks had passed, and the camp's situation became more worrisome as the death toll increased. Some women, including Diana, Sara, and Deborah, stood by an open mule cart on this particular day. About ten deceased children were lying face-up on the ground by the cart. Several British soldiers pick up the dead children. They unceremoniously threw the corpses of children in the cart. The Boer mothers wept at the sight of their dead children being thrown into the cart. Diana had tears, and her white habit was becoming rather dirty. Joseph, Deborah's son, was among the dead. A British corporal named Phillips picked up little Joseph. Suddenly, Deborah ran toward Phillips with clenched fists.

"No! Don't you, dear, take my little Joseph."

She struck Phillips several times as she attempted to pull her departed child away from his grasp. Suddenly, British corporals Jones and Woodson rush toward Deborah, carrying their rifles on their shoulders. They pull her away from Phillips. Woodson managed to apply a hold on Deborah. However, Deborah put up a struggle.

"Let me go, you damn filthy animal! Let me go!"

Jones retrieved his rifle and raised his arms as if to strike Deborah with the butt end of the weapon.

Diana stepped in. "Stop! I command you to stop!"

Jones turned and looked at Diana.

"And why should I?"

"Because it is in your heart to do so. You just do not know how to."

Jones looked confused. Diana reached and gently touched his arm, smiling. She guided his arms downward. Jones said nothing as his rifle was lowered. Her touch spellbound him.

Diana then addressed Woodson. "You can let her go now. All she requires is to hold her dead little child one last time."

Woodson nodded. "Sure, Sister."

He let go of Deborah, who retaliated by kicking Woodson in the leg.

"Ouch! That bitch kicked me."

Deborah immediately went to retrieve dead Joseph. Phillips prevented her by holding her back.

"Please let her go."

"Sister. We have strict orders not to let any Boer touch their deceased."

"If that were your son, I am sure you would desire to hold him just one more time."

"Sister!"

"Please."

Phillips reluctantly let Deborah go. Deborah picked up deceased Joseph and held him to her chest. She continued weeping as her tears landed on the dirty face of her deceased son.

Diana addressed Phillips. "Thank you."

A short time later, a mule driver led the cart to the burial site. However, the cart was empty. A small group of British soldiers carried the dead Boer children. Each soldier carried a deceased child, except for a few mothers who decided to carry their own. Diana was walking between Deborah and Sara with her arms around them. Even Jones and Woodson carried a deceased child, while Phillips carried Joseph. Every soldier appeared to have a somber look painted on their faces.

CHAPTER 10 – A WAY FORWARD

It was June 17, 1901, and the streets of downtown London were busy as people walked about. A young paperboy was standing on a street corner selling the daily edition of the "London Times." "Come here for your London Times! That's right! Your London Times! Here!"

The paper headline screamed: "PARLIAMENT TO DEBATE THE CAMPS."

The paper boy continued. "House of Commons to discuss the camps in South Africa!"

A gentleman dressed in a suit walked up and purchased an edition from the boy.

Parliament was in full session in the Common Chamber inside the House of Commons. As usual, the party representing the Government, including Prime Minister Lord Salisbury and his cabinet, sat on one side, while the Opposition party sat directly on the other. Lord Salisbury and his cabinet sat on the front bench nearest the chamber's center.

Parliament Member Sir Henry Campbell-Bannerman was speaking as he addressed Secretary of War Sir John Brodrick, sitting next to the Prime Minister, Lord Salisbury.

"…I wonder how long the House of Commons is going to endure this. It may, perhaps, excite some strange feeling amongst us to know that these camps of Boer women and children are surrounded by fences of barbed wire, but there is a barbed wire fence around the House of Commons, which prevents us exercising the ordinary rights of speech which belong to this Assembly. So much, Sir, for the motion which has been made. The whole question is two-fold, and I confess, one that the part to which my honorable friend confines the attention of the House, although eminently urgent and deserving of attention, cannot, I think, be discussed without reference to the other portion, and that other portion we are precluded from discussing."

Campbell-Bannerman then addressed Lord Salisbury, Prime Minister of Great Britain. "What I object to is the whole policy of concentration, the whole policy of destroying the homes of women and children, driving them in circumstances of considerable cruelty, certainly of unintentional cruelty, into these camps."

Lord Salisbury looked at Campbell-Bannerman with a blank stare, as members of the Opposition party momentarily cheered in agreement.

Campbell-Bannerman continued. "Under the very natural and proper ruling of the Speaker, we cannot discuss the whole of that side of the question, and what we have, therefore, to speak on is merely the condition of those camps. Now,

Sir, I have not seen the report of Mr. Rowntree, long a respected Member of this House, but I am acquainted with the reports of the gallant and plucky lady Emily Hobbouse who went out to South Africa in order to do what benefit she could to these unfortunate people; and I wish to say this. I am confirmed in my belief in the accuracy of her reports because of their most remarkable fairness. She brings no accusation, and I am sure that none of us would do so—at least, speaking for myself, I have never said a word that would imply cruelty or even indifference on the part of officers or men in the British Army."

Campbell-Bannerman then surveys the members. "It is the whole system which they have to carry out that I consider, to use a word which I have already applied to it, barbarous. There are no people in the world who feel that barbarity more than the unfortunate men whose duty it is to enforce that very system."

Members of the Government stood to their feet and jeered at Campbell-Bannerman. Lord Salisbury stood and shouted at him. The jeering continued, as some members from the Opposition party stood to their feet and yelled back. The Speaker of the House, presiding over the session, banged his gavel to call for order, as both parties continued to shout at each other. Henry Campbell-Bannerman grinned with the reaction he hoped for, as the debate continued.

Eight months had passed since the Parliament debate, and events had drastically changed at Bloemfontein camp. Diana was now a nurse again at the hospital as she walked, making her rounds. She was cheerful, and her white habit was immaculately clean. The atmosphere was quite different now, as the patients in their cots appeared in good spirits. Emaciation seemed to be gone from the hospital. The malnutrition that had plagued the camp had been lifted, as the British government had taken drastic action to better care for the Boer women and children.

Diana approached a nine-year-old Boer patient named Barbara as she sat in her cot. With her lengthy hair, she was enjoying her bowl of soup and a glass of orange juice, both sitting on a tray. Barbara was covered with measles.

Diana momentarily touched her forehead. "How are you doing this fine morning, Barbara?"

"I'm doing fine, Diana."

"Good. Your temperature appears normal. Before you know it, those measles will be gone."

"I hope so."

"Oh, they will. Just wait and see."

Barbara smiled at Diana as she put a spoonful of soup into her mouth. Diana stroked her long hair. Suddenly, Shaka and Elandria walked up to Diana.

"Well, hello, my children."

Shaka addressed Diana. "Diana, do you want us

to wash the linen now?"

"After lunch."

Diana approached a nearby open window, and Shaka and Elandria followed. She observed some British soldiers completing a small water well. She then observed some Boer women and children milling about on a lovely sunny day.

Diana turned to the children. "A sergeant I spoke to the other day informed me the well shall be ready tomorrow."

Elandria asked, "Does that mean we will have another well?"

"It sure does. God has plenty of water under the ground for us to use."

A cheer came over the faces of Shaka and Elandria.

"Come, let's take a walk." Diana went back to Barbara's bed. "I will see you soon."

"Okay, Diana."

Diana walked away as Shaka and Elandria followed close behind. Suddenly, she encountered British doctor Stanley Logan, who was in his forties.

"Doctor. Can I have your permission to take a short break with Shaka and Elandria?"

"Why sure, Diana. I believe we can manage." Stanley smiled at the children. "Why hello, Shaka and Elandria. How is everything?"

Shaka and Elandria answered together. "Fine, doctor."

"Glad to hear it." Stanley began to leave but

decided to stop. "Oh, by the way, Diana. The quinine you requested will arrive the day after tomorrow. As well as another shipment of calcium chloride."

"Thank you, doctor."

"You know Diana. You are a blessing here. I do not know what we would have done without you."

"I am only fulfilling my duty."

Stanley smiled at Diana and walked away. Diana continued to walk out with Shaka and Elandria.

They step outside the hospital as they continue their walk through the campgrounds. Dutch children run and play about. Like the hospital, the signs of emaciated children were nowhere to be found. A few Dutch women planted a small flower garden by their tents. Diana walked beside Shaka and Elandria.

Shaka asked, "What day is this?"

"Why the seventeenth day of February?"

Elandria proudly answered, "And the year of nineteen hundred and two."

"Good for you, Elandria."

"I told her that," Shaka explained.

"Well, siblings should be helping each other." Diana found a nearby bench, and all three sat, with Shaka and Elandria beside each other. "Children. It appears that this war will finally end soon."

Excitement in Shaka's eyes, "Really!"

"Yes. And I thought how wonderful it would be if you both wanted to see Ireland."

Elandria looked confused, "You mean like visit?"

Shaka nodded, "Yes, sister."

"What I was referring to is more of a permanent basis." They looked at Diana with wide-eyed curiosity. Diana responded with a reassuring smile. "How would you both think about living in Ireland?"

Shaka could not believe what he was hearing. "Really!"

Elandria was also startled. "That is for real?"

"Yes, it is."

Shaka still did not understand. "Who would take care of us?"

"I would. As my children. Provided I receive permission, since your parents are deceased."

Elandria is all smiles. "That sounds fine by me."

"Can nuns do that?"

"Well, actually, no, Shaka. Nuns are not allowed to have children of their own."

"How come you can?"

"Because I decided to leave the sisterhood." Diana reflected for a moment. "I promised to stay long enough in the sisterhood to see a change in my life. But the love I experienced with someone made me realize changes must be made now. And one of them is to leave the sisterhood."

Shaka and Elandria stared at Diana with blank looks on their face.

Diana smiled back at them. "I know you both do not understand. But one day, when you both become older, you shall. I did arrive with other sisters."

Shaka asked, "Where are they?"

"They already sailed back to Ireland and are doing well except for Sister Helen, who is no longer with the living. She died several weeks ago. The news was rather hard for me. But we all must face our death one day, just like we all must face the possibility of making important changes in our lives." Diana noticed confusion registered on their faces. "Don't worry. My devotion to God will never change." She patted their heads. "So, you both want to live with me?"

Shaka and Elandria answered in unison. "Sure!"

Diana leaned over and kissed them both on the cheeks.

On May 31, 1902, the Treaty of Vereeniging was signed in Pretoria, ending the Second Boer War. This meant both Boer republics would be under British rule. However, the republics were granted self-government as British colonies. The treaty also allowed for the amnesty of the Boer commandos and provided £3 million to reconstruct the Transvaal, known as the South African Republic.

In downtown Johannesburg, a young lad sold the daily edition of "The Star, Johannesburg Transvaal". He barked with paper in his raised hand," The war is over. The war is over!"

The following caption is read: "WAR IS OVER-

PEACE TREATY SIGN AT PRETORIA."

The lad continued, "Come read for yourself." Several people rushed over to the Lad and purchased newspapers.

Fireworks exploded in the air. Various people dance in the streets to the happy news.

A week later, on a beautiful day in the port of Durban, South Africa, a lovely British propeller ship, approximately 600 feet long, was ready to sail to Europe. It was a two-funnel steam engine. The passengers on board were military officers, British civilians, and medical volunteers.

Many passengers stood on the ship's deck railing, waving to the people on port side. Diana, Shaka, and Elandria stepped away from the railing. Diana wore a traditional cotton dress, with her hair shining in the sunlight. Shaka and Elandria wore new clothes, according to the tradition of children living in Europe. Diana also wore Juan's diamond necklace. They began to walk away.

Shaka admired the necklace. "Is that necklace from Ireland?"

Diana momentarily touched the necklace. "No. I received it from someone I love dearly. His name was Juan, and I worked with him at the hospital. We became very close friends."

Elandria seems puzzled. "Why is he not here?"

"He died." Suddenly, Diana stopped walking. Sadness was written on her face.

Unexpectedly, Elandria looked up and pointed

to the blue sky. "Look! A rainbow."

A beautiful rainbow appeared out of nowhere and stretched endlessly. It was as if the rainbow was leading the ship back to Ireland. Diana began to shed tears as she bent over to hug the children.

"Thank you, Lord. For ending this dreadful war. For allowing me to meet and fall in love with Juan. And having these two beautiful children."

The ship pulled away from the harbor. People still waved to each other from the port. The ship sailed as if following the rainbow.

ABOUT THE AUTHOR

Mark Ingle

I am married with three children. My contracting duties currently occupy most of my working time.

The idea for "Where My Heart Leads Me" came from my fascination with how mixing Faith, Love, and War can create potent storytelling. Although love and war appear to be quite different, they share some similarities. They both involve intense emotions, a desire for conquest, and sometimes the justification of extreme actions to achieve a goal. Each involves strategies, tactics, and the drive to win.

Individuals often seek stronger emotional bonds during times of crisis, such as war, leading to intense emotional relationships. The emotional tragedy of war can foster such emotional bonds.

Faith is also an interesting topic, as it has played a significant role in wars. Faith in God can offer justifications for creating wars. Religious leaders can also emphasize non-violence and forgiveness, and mediate for peace. Besides motivational factors for wars and peace, faith can cause conflict in the human heart. It can create a struggle of the heart when emotional love develops between two people.

Therefore, an internal war within the person develops regarding which side to take—a faith of devotion with sexual abstinence or the passion that sensual love can offer. Through research on the Second Boer War, I explain how faith, love, and war connections can create powerful emotional and complex forces of ethical and moral conflicts in times of war.

I have also written several other projects in different genres, including "The Wave Master".

Printed in Dunstable, United Kingdom